SHORELINE OF INFINITY

A...
fic...
in...
U...

CW01466246

ISSUE 37:
SPRING 2024

ISSN: 2059-2590
ISBN: 978-1-7395359-1-9

Submissions of fiction, art, reviews, poetry, non-fiction are welcomed: visit the website to find out how to submit

www.shorelineofinfinity.com

Publisher
Shoreline of Infinity Publications /
The New Curiosity Shop
Edinburgh
Scotland

180324

Co-founders:
Noel Chidwick,
Mark Toner

Fiction Editor:
Eris Young

Reviews Editor:
Ann Landmann

Non-fiction Editor:
Pippa Goldschmidt

Production Editors:
Noel Chidwick,
Andrew Lyndsay

Copy-editors: Pippa
Goldschmidt
Iain Maloney
Eris Young
Cat Hellisen

EDITORIAL TEAM

CONTENTS

COVER ART
Scribble Imp

FIRST CONTACT
www.shorelineofinfinity.com
contact@shorelineofinfinity.com
Twitter: @shoreinf
Also on Instagram & Bluesky

PULL UP A LOG

Life can feel a little gloomy at the moment for us sci-fi types in Scotland; our favourite arts council Creative Scotland (they've funded us twice here at Shoreline Towers) has just announced that it must cut its funding by 10%, and we're waiting to see what effects these cuts will have on an already struggling arts sector. To put this in context, the average income of a writer in the UK has decreased from £12,000 in 2007 to £7000 in in 2022, and less than a fifth of us are able to make a living solely from our writing. In the absence of fairy godmothers we need sources of funding if we're to continue to produce stories.

News from abroad also continues to appal; how else to respond to it than with visions of alternative worlds, or satirical take-downs of cruel realities? Yasmin Kanaan's non-fiction essay on Palestinian SF introduces us to some classic texts.

The stories in this issue respond to a number off frightening realities, from inequalities in access to healthcare to the implications of AI and data mining to the creative industries. The stories respond with anger, humour, absurdity and escapism, but they each have something to say.

Perhaps we have a duty to search for the upbeat, to not succumb to despair. Emma Levin's essay reminds us that SF – particularly when mutated into horror – and comedy frequently go hand-in-hand, providing plenty of laughs and reminding us to find humour where we can. Marc Criley's flash fiction piece about alien pets brings much needed warmth and levity to an otherwise heavy issue. Ruth E J Booth's column takes us into the forest where the boundary between reality and fiction has always been blurred.

What's more, we have real life events to look forward to. The first rays of Glasgow's WorldCon are already visible over the horizon. And Cymera...

—The Editorial Team

The Commute of the Valkyries

Rebecca Zahabi

You **download the form** from an official-looking website. The printer is old, it spits and splutters the words, and you have to push down each blank page so its little teeth can catch it. Its teeth are blunted – more often than not, it can't eat the paper you feed it.

It prints each letter as sharp as runes. The title first: *Application for admission into the Valhöll.* The detail next: *To be used by men in the Channel Islands, Isle of Man and British overseas territories, if destined to die in battle, for Einherjar duties; and by women who live elsewhere for Valkyrie duties.* Destinies and duties are different for men and women, even in the afterlife. You know that much. You watch as the printer spits out line after line, reading upside-down, craning your neck.

The instructions on the form are brief.

The ash Yggdrasill is of all trees best.
Keep this information for further reference.

You keep this information for further reference.

It is a bright summer day outside; the office is cramped and dark. The form is written in small, intricate lines, so you go outside to find some light.

There is an ash tree growing by the road beside your workplace. You sit below the tree to fill in the form; you struggle writing against your legs, you should have taken a book to rest the pen against, it rips through the thin paper.

You look up at the tree for comfort. The ash is of all trees best, but this one is gangly and gnarled, manky and mangy; the leaves gape, spotted with air pollution, like a mouth without enough teeth.

You sit in the shade of Yggdrasill and complete the form. Cars drive by. You imagine your lungs like the leaves, green and red on the inside, dappled with black and grey, sticky patches like on the photographs at the back of cigarette packs. You breathe in the exhaust fumes until it makes you dizzy. You wonder why you never smoked. It seems like such a waste of lungs.

But then, smoke would damage your teeth.

The form includes a warning at the end: *Serious or fatal crushing injuries can occur.*

You tick the box which says you consent to the risks. You push up the form against the tree trunk to sign it, and your signature is wobbly on the bark.

It needs to be scanned and emailed back to them. You head back inside the office.

While you struggle with the scanner in the staff room, you wonder why they didn't have an online application process. It would have been easier. Maybe easier isn't the point.

The scanner has a mouth of raw gums and square glowing lines. It swallows your paper. It never chokes on what it's given.

Creatures around you, you realise, don't have enough teeth.

It takes time to do the scan. You place each page, one side up, scan, turn the page around manually, the other side, scan, next page, scan, turn that one around, scan.

While you wait, you wonder if being a Valkyrie becomes as dreary as scanning forms. You picture the foamy floaty drink, taken from the udder of the magical goat who gives beer instead of milk, the cup filled with creamy liquid gold, placed on the table for the warriors to quaff. The clunk of horn on wood. Then udder, beer, horn, table. Rinse and repeat.

As through a grimy mirror, you see your future silhouette draped in furs and leather, the heavy pieces of ceremonial armour across your shoulders, chatting with the other Valkyries queuing for the goat, the same comments as for the scanner.

"Gods she's slow today. Capricious."

"Why won't the third teat give, do you know?"

"Press the udder harder."

"Have you tried scratching between her shoulders?"

"The poor thing's sore. Give her a break."

"I wish they would give me a break."

There is the slight brush of the ceremonial office skirt against your thighs.

The scanner whizzes and whirrs; you wonder what sound a goat makes. In the Valhöll, the warriors drink from horns in one go, then place them upside-down on the table. You cannot put down a half-finished drink if it's served in a horn. You know that much.

As a Valkyrie, you'll rub your wrists circled with gold and think of the scanner, how it was artificial yet had a temper. You'll say to the others, "For the scanner, the best moment to use it was during sunny afternoons, because nothing makes people avoid scanners like sunny afternoons."

It will occur to you, then, that you might also want to avoid goats on lazy afternoons.

"You know," another woman will say, her thick white arms like rising dough, "you know, the Celts are better if you're a woman. More female gods. More fertility rituals with lots of steamy sex."

Another, with hair so red it must be dyed with blood, she'll say, "Still, better than the Greeks." Everyone nods. Still better than the Greeks. The rate of sexual harassment if you're a nymph is off the chart. Plus, there's a victim-blaming culture there. Look at Medusa.

In the office that blocks out the afternoon light, one of your colleagues comes to talk to you. He says, "I have something to scan." He shows you.

It's a drawing of two humanoid flowers. They have smiles between their petals. One is blue and one is pink. There are little hearts in the air. The blue flower is holding two human heads on spikes and offering them to the pink one. The pink one seems flattered. The caption above it reads: *In an alternative universe.*

He doesn't realise that you are the sort of woman who puts human heads on spikes and gifts them to the gods.

He says, "It's funny, isn't it?"

You don't say this has nothing to do with work. You assume he knows. Anyway, your form has nothing to with work.

He says, "I thought you would find it funny. It's your kind of humour."

You don't want to talk, because you know that for him talking is flirting, but you admit that yes, this is your kind of humour. Kind of.

"Because of the joke you made," he says. "About the departed."

You do not remember making jokes.

"You could depart now," you say.

Your teeth are blunted; he doesn't depart. You are only halfway through the form and cannot leave the scanner.

When you leave, he follows. He didn't need to scan the flowers. He only brought them out to show you. He is under the mistaken impression that you are harmless, therefore desirable. You take the lift with your colleague. It is an unlucky place to be. It is an unlucky person to be with.

The lift stalls.

"It does that sometimes," he says. "It happens. If we just..." He leans awkwardly over you to reach the control panel. "Yes, if we just click this, it's a switch that if we... Normally that should do it."

He has pressed a button, but nothing has happened. You wait. Nothing happens.

"This normally does it," he says. He presses the button again.

"We should call for help," you say.

He presses the button again. You move away from him. The lift is too narrow, and your colleague is big and broad and sweaty. He wipes his fingers against his trousers.

"I don't think there's a help button," he says. "Normally this does it, I don't know why it isn't working."

There are always help buttons in elevators, so you can be extracted from this long metallic throat. You think of flowers which digest flies in their acids, closing in on the insect. You are an insect and the walls are closing in on you.

Why do flowers have teeth if they don't need to chew?

"It's funny, isn't it, stuck together here," he says. "Something to laugh about later. To tell the kids."

"You have kids?" you ask.

"No." He presses the button again. "No, it's just something you say, don't you, to tell the kids later, maybe if... One day I might have kids."

You doubt it.

"We should call for help," you repeat. Maybe your life is an elevator with no help button, only unhelpfully helpful colleagues and helpfully unhelpful forms. "Using a phone." You left your mobile upstairs. Where you were going, you

didn't need it.

"I'm not sure the network goes through the lift's doors," he says, pulling his phone out of his trouser pocket. "They're too thick, I think."

He laughs. You consider gifting him to the gods. You are not sure his sacrifice is worthy enough to unblock the elevator, so you refrain from it. He would dislike you, if he heard your thoughts. Sometimes, you wish your dreams were louder.

"Still, a funny story to tell later, if not to the children, then the wife."

"You have a wife?" you ask.

"No."

A lifetime away from now, you will be riding across the skies, and you will see a dead soul glinting, and your colleague will raise his hands, begging to be taken to the hall of warriors. You will remember, suddenly, your joke about the departed. You will notice, for the first time, that he had a kindness about him, a softness, which did not prevent him from being cruel. Destinies and duties are different for men and women. When you'll turn away, you will feel sorry.

You do not know what happens to those who do not drink beside the gods. You imagine they are doomed to scanning forms for the underworlds.

You need to go to the Valhöll before you turn into a thing without teeth which never chokes on what it's given. You yearn to have bite.

It is nine days before they answer. Three days is the norm for European fairy tales, but in places with sunrises as long as days and dusks as long as nights, nine is the magic number.

Your application has been taken into consideration. You have an appointment.

You carefully follow the instructions on how to prepare for the interview. *Flute the edges and brush with beaten egg.* You flute your edges, pinch them down, take away your sharpness. You brush beaten egg across your skin until it glows. When it is time to go, you aren't sure whether clothes would scrape away the egg. You go naked.

There was a woman the colour of gold who once went naked before the gods. They tried to burn her, but the egg was too wet to catch fire, and she breathed in and exhaled the smoke with lungs which were burnished by exhaust fumes from cars. You know that much.

They do not try to burn you. They ask the usual interview questions; what is your greatest achievement, what are your strengths in the workplace, why are you the right fit for them, if you were a part of the human body, what would you be?

You do not want to answer teeth, in case they think you proud.

"I'd be a woman's Adam's apple," you say. They frown. "Women have them too. They're called the laryngeal prominence." You don't see why only men should have apples. "It could be called Eve's fig," you say. A fig is smaller than an apple. You'll grant them that.

They do not like the answer. Maybe they don't like mixing mythologies. Idunn has apples too, and she was once transformed into a walnut. Maybe you should have talked about Idunn's walnuts, rather than mention Eve.

As you give answers, a realisation strikes. You want teeth and wings, armour and power over the fallen. But you do not want the binds they have to offer. You listen to the future conversations you will have around the magic goat. The half-whispered words of envy.

"Look at the Jötnar, the giants living wild beyond the borders. Look at Utgard-Loki, in his shapeshifting palace fit to trick a god."

The women will shake their heads and click their tongues.

"No pay."

"No comfort."

"Too risky."

They will straighten their helmets, wipe the horns clean around the rims. They'll return to the tables with full cups, leaving you thoughtful behind, resting one hand against the goat's withers.

"But still. To live beyond the walls," you'll whisper.

You'll consider the ways the Jötnar thrive. Murder. Drink. Make merry. Dance. Skadi divorced her husband. Gjalp peed in a river until it overflowed in an attempt to drown her enemies. Angrboda raised children who would devour the world.

There is a lot you could do besides serve.

At the end of the interview they are pleased, despite the blunder about Eve. "At least you didn't mention Lilith," they joke. No-one likes a woman who turns into a monster rather than following orders. "You'll like the job. It fits your kind of mindset."

You don't want to agree, because you know that for them asserting is winning, but you admit that yes, this is your kind of mindset. Kind of.

They tell you that in the Valhöll, the women carry the dead on wings like birds split open. They do not tell you that the women serve drinks for the men and never die. You do not need a paradise of serving drinks and never dying, but you know how to conduct yourself in an interview. Your colleague who didn't depart would be proud. You tick all the boxes.

They are convinced. Like all rituals, it is painful. Like all transformations, it is necessary. They sever your ribs from your spine, remove your lungs, and carve the wings of the blood eagle on your back

Now you can fly. It is a long commute up Yggdrasill to the canopy where the gods built their halls. Serious or fatal crushing injuries can occur in *Fraxinus excelsior*'s branches.

Now you can breathe. And bite.

With wings, you can crest above the walls and go beyond. You'll wonder, afterwards, what took you so long.

You fly, but not towards the Valhöll.

Rebecca Zahabi (she/her) is a Sunday Times bestselling author of speculative fiction. Her short stories have appeared in *The Magazine of Fantasy & Science-Fiction* and PodCastle. The third and final volume of her epic fantasy trilogy, *The Lightborn*, is coming out in May 2024. Aside from writing traditional fiction, she also writes for video games.

'The Commute of the Valkyries' is partly inspired by 'Viking Dublin: Trial pieces' by Seamus Heaney and its moody, atmospheric take on old Norse myths.

KNOCK KNOCK!! KNOCK'

DON'T YOU CAER ABOUT US HUMNS?

Generative Leaf-Mould Transformer

Vikram Ramakrishnan

"Let an ultraintelligent machine be defined as a machine that can far surpass all the intellectual activities of any man however clever... Thus the first ultraintelligent machine is the last invention that man need ever make... "
—Irving John Good, British mathematician and cryptologist

G autam rummaged through Post-its atop his desk for the quote. It was a great quote. No, it was the *perfect* quote for his autonomous vehicles story. He had interviewed an industry visionary who called programmatic trucking a "pathway to human *something*." But Gautam forgot that particular *something*, and he needed it because it brimmed with brilliance.

"Batavia," a voice behind him boomed.

He swiveled around in his chair and tugged at his shirt's hem. Maurice, the sharp-nosed editor-in-chief of *The City Times,* was leaning against Gautam's cubicle. He squeezed a ball of silly putty and then smashed it between his palms.

"I need you," Maurice said.

"For what?" Gautam said.

"An interview."

"Who?"

"L.M. Michon."

Gautam started. L.M. Michon, by far the most famous author of his generation? Michon had never done an interview before. Ever. Sixty years of books, and his output hadn't even slowed. Over time, it had soared.

"L.M. Michon?" Gautam asked.

"Yeah, I know," Maurice said, tossing the disk of silly putty into the air. "This is huge."

"It's not even my beat. Shouldn't someone from *Arts & Letters* take it?"

"No, it's got to be you. Michon's PR person was adamant about that," Maurice said. "Someone's got a fan."

"And I thought only my mom read my stories."

"You'll meet with Abel Carlson today. He's the one who contacted us. I'll send you the address."

"Today?"

"We want to drop this feature Monday. Stories like this are why *The City Times* exists. This will be one of the biggest interviews of your career. Don't mess this one up."

"I won't," Gautam said, meaning it.

Several years ago, on Gautam Batavia's sixteenth birthday, his grandfather took him to the City Library. Three grand marble arches greeted them as they climbed steep stairs. Between these arches stood a pair of columns running from the ground to the roof, where carved heads of lions gave off an impression of refinement as if endowed with the gift of literacy. Miss Trellis, the Chief Librarian, was waiting for them when they arrived. She was an older woman with a small face and tortoise-shell eyeglasses, dressed in a white cardigan over her turquoise dress.

"Happy Birthday, Gautam," she said, patting his hand. "Are you ready to see the special collection?"

"It's your present," his grandfather said. "I hope you enjoy it."

They followed Miss Trellis to the back of the library, an enormous hall with long wooden tables, patrons reading in silence. Gautam had never visited the library before; he preferred to pirate books from the Net and then read them on his eReader. He devoured books so quickly he claimed he didn't need to buy them.

"Who is your favorite author, Gautam?" Miss Trellis asked, striding ahead, her heels clicking on the floor.

"L.M. Michon," Gautam blurted out.

"Michon?" Miss Trellis laughed, peering over her shoulder. "You have quite an eclectic taste."

Gautam glanced at his smiling grandfather, shoved his hands into his pockets. At the back of the library, a plastic box hung next to a glass door, and Miss Trellis lifted its top and reached in. She handed Gautam latex gloves, plastic shoe coverings, and a shower cap.

"Put these on," she said, scanning her card. With a click, the door opened up to a white space. A burst of air conditioning hit Gautam. The ceiling gleamed with fluorescent light, flashing on a rectangular metal island in the center of the space. Miss Trellis entered a code on an attached tablet, two panes on the island slid open, and from this rose a pedestal with a brown leather-bound book atop it. Miss Trellis picked up the book and offered it to Gautam. L.M. Michon's *The Printing Press*. Gautam held the book with reverence.

"Open it," she said.

On the title page, under the large font letters, scrawled a looping signature stretching across the page.

"No way," he whispered.

Miss Trellis nodded. "The only known book signed by him."

Gautam traced a fingertip over the signature. He closed his eyes and imagined himself being a writer like Michon, signing the air in a flourish. His eyes shot open. "You know why I love him?"

Miss Trellis shook her head.

"Because in all his stories, even though the world keeps changing, his characters fight to be their best selves," Gautam said. "No matter what's happening."

"I thought this would give you some inspiration," his grandfather said. "Happy Birthday, Gautam."

"I want to be a writer like him one day," Gautam said, closing the book's cover.

He never pirated books again. They were too precious.

The experience sent Gautam on a writing fury. He became a reporter for his high school newspaper, and when he started at City University, he joined their paper too. During vacations he dithered with ideas for novels, but journalism seemed to be the only writing he could see through. The idea of summer after graduation excited him since he would finally have time to finish his novel.

One afternoon while at home, he browsed his room's bookshelf. He pulled out a copy of *The Printing Press* and sat down at his desk. He placed the book to his left. To his right was his notebook. With meticulous detail, he copied over a scene from Michon's novel into his notebook.

In this scene, the protagonist prince – who has so far followed the guidance of ancestral law – feels conflicted about his royal family after the invention of the printing press. His family wants the printing press destroyed because it allows the printing of blasphemy and can sow chaos. The scene sets the rest of the story into motion. The prince initially turns against his family. But in the end, he is able to convince his family how the world has changed and how they too, must change with it. The prince's diligent work heralds a new age.

Gautam focused on the moments in the story that triggered emotion in him. He took a highlighter to Michon's word choices. He underlined passages that twisted his insides. Soon, so rapt, he tossed his highlighter on the table and leaned back, throwing his feet onto his desk.

A knock came at his door.

"What?" Gautam yelled, "I'm in the middle of the creative process."

The knocking continued unabated and amplified.

Gautam slammed the book upside down on his desk and opened the door. Jay, his younger brother, grinned, dimples denting his cheeks. He pulled his mouth wide open with his index fingers, and stuck his tongue out.

"Go away," Gautam said, gritting his teeth, shutting the door.

When he sat back down, the knocking started again.

"Leave me alone!" he screamed. "I need to concentrate!"

The knocks and giggles didn't stop.

Gautam stood at his door gripping the knob tightly, his neck and ears hot with blood. He gritted his teeth, shoved the door, and chased after Jay. The two scrambled down the hall, Jay laughing, until Gautam suddenly dove for Jay, his arms wrapping around his legs. Jay slipped and slammed his head against the wall. Gautam screamed for his parents to call an ambulance. For a moment, Jay glared at Gautam before his eyelids fluttered, and his eyes rolled to the back of his head. Gautam cradled Jay in his arms.

"I'm so sorry," he said. "I didn't mean to do that."

An ambulance arrived, sirens piercing, rushing Jay to the hospital. There, doctors and nurses moved with urgent precision, Gautam and his parents in pursuit. A CT scan revealed a brain bleed. The doctors said if it weren't for the hospital's new scanning machine, the family could have lost Jay. The good news was that he would recover with medication and regular imaging. Gautam's parents hugged, both sobbing into each other's arms while he stood with his back against the wall, hoping to be unseen, the weight of guilt pressing down on him.

Gautam didn't write a word for the rest of the summer.

That fall, Gautam joined *The City Times* as a junior technology reporter. He thought the discipline would help his punctuated fiction career, but he quickly learned he didn't have enough time.

As new modes of extracting value from silicon bloomed, Gautam reported on them: machines flying the skies on their own; the ethical implications of programmatic biological mods; and, most recently, the effects of artificial intelligence on corporate supply chains.

His inbox overflowed with messages from PR teams angling for client coverage, tech startups that had all apparently solved poverty and world hunger. One email subject read, "Our automation AI solution has cured inequality. Here's a calendar invite to discuss."

Other emails arrived as intimidations. One man threatened Gautam's life if he did not stop his reporting. The email subject read, "DON'T YOU CAER ABOUT US HUMNS?"

Gautam often felt compelled to respond. He thought that rationally explaining automation's benefits – it would free people to be more creative – would quell his detractors. He spent hours crafting various replies, but seldom received a follow-up email. If an answer came, it would arrive with three words in the body: "Go to hell."

Time had become precious, and the moments to work on his novel-in-perpetual-progress disappeared. Meeting Michon would give Gautam much-needed inspiration. Maybe the author would impart writing advice too.

Michon's home was a simple brownstone on the west side of the city. Black metal railings bracketed the brownstone's ruddy facade. Purple and maroon flowers alternated in small pots up the steps. In front of the door, letters and magazines littered the ground. They were all addressed to Abel Carlson.

Gautam was disappointed; he thought he was visiting Michon's home, but instead, he was at the PR person's. Michon must be so secretive he didn't want anyone to know where he lived. What other secrets did the author have?

He pressed the doorbell, scooped up an armful of mail, and waited for the door to open. He had so many questions for Michon. How did he maintain such a consistent output for so long? What would his next book be about? Why did he want to be interviewed now?

The door scraped open. A wrinkled man with white hair sat in a motorized wheelchair. He wore a white and black striped sweater and thick lenses housed in circular black wireframes sat on his nose.

"Gautam?" he asked, a faint wheezing in his voice. He rolled closer, and the sunlight lit his face. His skin was pink as if he had been sunbathing for too long. "You didn't have to do that," he said, gesturing to the mail with a frail, almost skeletal arm. "I'm so absent-minded. Thank you for bringing it in."

He reversed his wheelchair back inside. The foyer smelled of warm wood and faint incense. A teak desk overflowed with mail, and behind it, family pictures covered a beige wall showing school events and graduations; one photo depicted an awkwardly grinning, yellow-shirted boy in a wheelchair. He was embracing a trophy in his lap and behind him stood a tall man with square glasses and a thick beard, his smile lighting up the picture.

Abel had a coughing fit. His body spasmed, and he extended an arm at an inhaler on the table. Gautam dropped the mail, grabbed the inhaler, and leapt to him. Abel took a deep breath from it, closed his eyes, and exhaled.

"Are you ok?" Gautam asked. "Should I get you water?"

"I'm fine. Thank you. I always forget this thing," Abel said, clutching the inhaler. "My emphysema acts up at the worst possible moments. Come, come. I have so much to share with you. Let's go to the library."

The library was an arch-roofed den with oak beams running the ceiling. On the walls, hundreds of built-in shelves heaved with books from paperbacks to leather-bound tomes with cracked spines.

"My father loved books," Abel said. "Come, sit."

He pointed to an argyle couch and coffee table. Behind him, a desk sat flush against the wall. Light drifted in the room from a French window above a large desktop computer, blue and green lights flashing on its face. Next to it was a wide monitor with a black screen and an inkjet printer.

"Your father?" Gautam said. He thought of the pictures on the foyer. "Your father is L.M. Michon?"

"He is in one way, but in another way," Abel said, gesturing to all the books around him. "We all are L.M. Michon."

"Sorry?"

"No, I'm the one to apologize. Look at me. Launching into it all before even offering you anything. Would you like some water? A drink? Single malt?"

"I'm all right," Gautam said, not meaning it. Something was off. A strange din started in his head.

"You're confused, that's okay."

"I thought I would interview your father."

Abel intertwined his fingers, placed his hands in his lap, licked his lips, and cleared his throat. "My father is dead."

Panic overwhelmed Gautam. He sat up quickly. "Dead?"

"He's been dead for almost twenty years."

"But—"

"How has so much work been coming out under his name?"

"Yes!" Gautam cried.

"I've been releasing it," Abel said, looking back at the computer screen. "With a little help."

Gautam noticed the gentle hum of the desktop. He waited for Michon to pop up on the screen or something just as ridiculous. He didn't know if he wanted to laugh or cry. Suddenly, the single malt sounded good.

"L.M. Michon was my father's pen name. His real name was Adam Carlson. He wasn't just a writer. He was also a computer programmer. Do you know why I contacted *The City Times* and asked for you?"

"I don't." Gautam looked down, not wanting to admit he thought Michon – no, this Adam Carlson – knew how big of a fan he was. He mumbled, "I thought you would want to speak with someone in *Arts and Letters*."

"Because you are a technology reporter," Abel said. "A very good one. The best, in fact. You imbue your stories with hope for progress."

Gautam looked up, his heart filling with pride.

"And this is a technology story. A story of progress. I'm about to show you the biggest technology story you will ever cover."

Abel began coughing again. Gautam stood up, and Abel shook his head while he took a breath from his inhaler. After rolling his wheelchair backward, he hit the spacebar and directed a confident gaze at Gautam. This time his smile, which had been calming, almost parental, was assured. It made Gautam uncomfortable.

"What topic did you write about last?" Abel asked.

"Ethical issues around long-haul trucking automation."

"What if I could let you write your article in a few seconds?"

"A few seconds? How?"

"Come meet GLMT."

Gautam stood next to him. The screen was white. At its center was the word 'TYPE,' and to its right, a cursor flashed.

He was overcome by impatience. He'd come to interview L.M. Michon. Instead, he learned the author was dead, and his son was publishing Michon's work posthumously. Now, he was trying to con him about a computer program of his. Was all this another elaborate startup ploy for coverage?

"GLMT - set 'type' to journalistic," Abel said.

The screen flashed green, revealing a new prompt reading 'STYLE.'

"'Style' - Gautam Batavia," Abel continued. "'Topic' - ethical issues surrounding long-haul trucking automation. 'Words' - five hundred. Print."

A few seconds later, the printer ran, and he handed Gautam its printout.

Gautam scanned the paper. Its argument followed the story he had been writing about the trucking industry. Some changes to transportation were inevitable, and because of their inevitability, the industry should embrace rather than revile them. Automation would accept the workload people would otherwise take on, allowing for more freedom, and in the end, creativity. It was a tad editorialized, as if Maurice had rephrased the sentences, but overall it was Gautam's voice. Then he saw a line containing the *something* he was looking for in his piles of notes that morning.

Automatic trucking was a pathway to human self-sovereignty.

That was the word he sought earlier in the day: *self-sovereignty.* It was the trucking visionary's quote – the expression bringing together the article. The paper felt fragile in Gautam's hands.

"H— how?" Gautam said.

"With GLMT," he said, patting the desktop. "Generative Leaf-Mould Transformer."

"Is this some kind of AI?"

"ASAL."

"ASAL?"

"Application-specific automatic learning," he said. "Statistics. Probabilities. Data wrangling. At the end of the day, it's all math. Decades of groundwork have finally come together because we now have the hardware."

"But, what about article research? Interviews? Fact-checking? You still need someone to do all that." Gautam asked. He paused. "Don't you?"

"GLMT does it," he said. "Corpora of internet data, chats, transcriptions of videos, political talks, and so on all feed the program. Its brain is an encyclopedia – if you want to think about it that way. It has the written, video, and oral history of humanity. And it's updated constantly."

Gautam scribbled furiously on his notepad. Excitement surged through him. What a game-changer. Once people had access to programmatic improvements, it would give them more time to work on their passions. Automation wasn't bad. It was another tool for humankind. If it could write his articles in seconds, it would give him so much more time to do other things like writing his novel.

"Technically," Abel said. "You don't even have to take notes."

Gautam stood for a second with his mouth agape. He was giddy. Then he laughed. This was amazing. Abel smiled and laughed with him. Gautam threw himself on the couch and tossed his notepad on the table.

"Incredible," he said. "What a piece of technology. Your father was such a huge inspiration, and now even more so. This kind of technology will free up the lives of so many people. I'm thinking about how I can write my novel now."

"You want to write a novel?" Abel asked.

Gautam nodded.

"GLMT writes fiction too," he said.

"What?" Gautam wiped happy wetness from his eyes.

"Did you think I was releasing my father's work, posthumously? That would be a lot of work."

Gautam looked down.

"I've been feeding GLMT corpora of his writing. Rough drafts," Abel continued. "Finished drafts. Things he never published. His diaries. Anything and everything that he wrote. And with that, it can produce work with my father's words and turns of phrase."

A wave of heat built in Gautam's stomach, and he realized he was clenching his jaw.

"That's why he created GLMT," Abel said. "Years ago, an author my father admired wrote about the 'leaf-mould' being everything that composed us. All our experiences. All our ideas. Everything we've read. Everything we've done. Everyone we've met," he said, padding his palms together like he was making a dough ball. "Everything forming us."

Heat ran up through Gautam's neck and over his ears. He felt queasy again.

"He became curious about this leaf-mould. Obsessed. My mother left him because of it," Abel said. "He began working on his prototype of GLMT, though he didn't have a name for it then. It was a kind of glorified auto-completer and thesaurus. When he fed it an idea or began a sentence, it would offer ten suggestions to choose from. A simple piece of software taking ages to run. Producing a five-hundred-word piece of work would take days. He could write it faster himself. 'Trivial and slow,' he called it once." He laughed, his eyes closed, looking up at the ceiling. "I miss his quips."

"Then you took over?" Gautam asked, impatient again.

"He was a good programmer and an excellent teacher," he said. He gestured to his legs. "Since I had nothing else to do with my time, I spent it learning about computers. I took the software up a few notches. The problem was programming only took us so far."

"What do you mean?"

"Hardware limitations. To make real inroads, we needed better hardware. And now we have it. Off-the-shelf GPUs are enough to accomplish what you saw here. People will need to curate their corpora to feed the software, of course. But, I can see open source communities flourishing by sharing corpora and tools," he said. "Imagine the Cambrian explosion of ideas when this is out in the open for anyone to use."

Gautam let out a long breath.

"I know," Abel said. "This is a lot to take in."

"Wait, wait." A vague horror crept through Gautam. "Did your father write any of his books when he was alive?"

"Of course. He wrote them."

Gautam sighed in relief.

"But if you mean without GLMT," Abel said. "Well, then that's a little trickier."

"So he didn't write *any* of them?" Gautam asked. He let impatience flood through his voice but he didn't care. He wanted Abel to hear it.

"Gautam, much like how you write with your computer now. He wrote them with the help of GLMT."

"That's cheating!"

"Cheating?" Abel's face bunched up like a raisin. "Cheating how?"

"Technology should give us – people – more time to be creative. It shouldn't be doing the creativity itself!"

"You still are being creative. You come up with creative ideas, and GLMT executes them. Imagine a world where anyone could tell their story. Someone who lives on the other side of the planet can tell us their stories. A blind child can write books about visually impaired protagonists captaining spaceships. GLMT can do all the research and make sure the science is right. Look at me, for example." Abel gestured to his legs. "Do I remind you of anyone?"

Michon's last protagonist had been a man in a wheelchair who also could fly. Critics called it an incredible, "genre-destructive" work by melting realism with the fantastic. It was so different from Michon's other books.

"See?" Abel continued. "I used GLMT to tell my story."

"This is different. Like you're taking the entire creation process away."

"I expected this kind of reaction. Think about this. What are we but not the product of those who came before us? Your writing is a product of all the journalists who came before you. Your research is the product of the research that came before it. GLMT takes it a step further."

Gautam had to think, to calm himself down. What if Abel was right, and he could use GLMT as Michon did – creating so many award-winning pieces of fiction? He nodded along as Abel

25

spoke; uttering all sorts of words, short words curling his lips into an 'o,' longer ones stretching them out into a wide grimace. The man's eyebrows rose, and his eyes crinkled as he laughed. Gautam matched his expressions, but Abel's words vanished in the ringing of his head. He felt like he was on a subway track with a train headed his way, and he couldn't do anything about it. Abel had tied his body to the tracks.

If everyone had access to GLMT, then how would anyone find him? He was unique – a brilliant writer who had just never had the time to write as much as he'd like to have.

It was unfair.

Unfair. Unfair. Unfair.

Gautam wanted to scream. Was any of this real?

"What's that?" Abel asked.

He started, not realizing he spoke aloud. He took a deep breath. "Did your father sign any books?"

"Like autographs?" Abel gave him a thin smile. "No, never. If you didn't realize, he was quite secretive."

"It's just that when . . . for my birthday. Never mind, it doesn't matter."

The book he saw at City Library was a forgery? None of this was real! It was all fake! There was no signature. There was no L.M. Michon. The man who wrote – if you can even call it writing – under his name had been dead for decades. And now, this? Abel wanted to take away from him the one thing he desired?

"This isn't right," Gautam said. "Some of us have worked for years on our novels. You can't just take that away from us."

"I'm not taking it away from you. GLMT will make your novel easier to finish. How is this different from what automation has done for other walks of life? Drone technology. Shipping. Transportation. What you have reported on."

"Those aren't creative industries! Writing is all about the creative process!" Gautam slammed a fist into his palm. "You can't automate it away!"

Abel stared at Gautam. His eyes were menacing, like he was a vulture waiting to strike.

"Perhaps I picked the wrong reporter to cover this," he said.

Gautam stood up, fists clenched. He was about to stomp out the door, and then Abel coughed, heaving into his fist. His noisy coughs filled the room. His arms shook as he pointed at the inhaler.

Gautam picked it up, looked at it carefully, and ran his thumb over its base. What if he could use GLMT for himself? No one else would have to know. He pulled the pod out of the inhaler and put it back in. He pressed down, and the inhaler let out a gust of medication, leaving the pod icy-cold. Wheezing sounds came from Abel.

He was old anyway. How much longer did he have? Gautam marched out of the room, shoving the inhaler into his pocket, and waited in the foyer. Through the glass, the alternating purple and maroon flowers looked like a surrealist painting. He thought about the Michon story, the one Maurice wanted. Gautam would have to come up with a cover story. There's no way he could let the world know about GLMT.

A sudden idea struck him. He could use GLMT to write a believable story. No one knew who L.M. Michon was, and no one needed to. This was going to be Michon's only interview ever.

The coughing continued, but Gautam ignored it. He looked at the pictures on the wall. In one a young Abel had a blue blanket covering his knees, and he held a stuffed rabbit. He was wearing a cap that had the Pi symbol on it. Gautam pulled the inhaler out of his pocket. He turned it over in his hands. What was he doing? Would he really let the man die? For what? He rushed into the den.

Abel's face was almost blue, his eyes were bulging, and he clutched at the air. Gautam shoved the inhaler in Abel's mouth, pressing down on the pod.

"Abel!" he screamed. "Breathe!"

The man wheezed in a breath that seemed to last forever. Afterward, his eyes closed, he slumped in his wheelchair, his head resting on his chest. He breathed quietly.

Gautam's heart flogged his insides, beating like thunder in a barrel drum. He wobbled backward and threw himself onto the couch. He felt like a small animal had crawled down his esophagus, scraped its claws on his insides, found its way into his stomach, curled up, and died.

Abel appeared to have no memory of the minutes leading up to his slumber. He seemed grateful for Gautam's help and even gave him an extra desktop stacked with the latest hardware to support GLMT. "You'll have a head start on everyone else," he said, giving him a wink as he left.

Gautam stood in Maurice's office in the corner while the editor read. A wall clock ticked loudly in the room, time seemingly moving away faster and faster. Suddenly, Maurice slammed the silly putty against his table and Gautam jumped.

"You're kidding me," Maurice said.

"I wish I was," Gautam said. "This is going to change everything."

"That's what technology does!" Maurice's voice boomed in the office. "You should be proud of your work. It will win awards."

And it did win awards. GLMT became the talk of the world. Once its software became open source, thousands of programmers built on top of its codebase, tinkering on their own versions. Quickly, books of all kinds, in all subjects, from everywhere exchanged hands. Kids from countries Gautam had never even heard of were producing best-sellers. Gautam's little brother Jay used GLMT to write a novel about a niche memory-related topic that was a hit in neuroscience circles. Gautam quickly realized he had to finally get to work on his novel, so he took a sabbatical from *The City Times*. Maurice told him he deserved it.

At his desk, for days, Gautam struggled getting words on the page. He tried reading L.M. Michon for inspiration, but the sentences were barely registering. The months passed quickly, the desktop with GLMT installed on it collecting dust in the corner of his room. After he got a call from Jay that his neuroscience novel had won an award, Gautam hung up, opened a new bottle of single malt, and stared at the machine. He took a drink and lugged the machine over, plugging it in. It hummed, as if asking him to use it. The screen prompted him to speak.

"GLMT," he said. "Let's write some pieces."

And GLMT created for him: twenty-five hundred words about artificially intelligent machinery; five thousand words on genetic manipulation; an alternate ending to Michon's *The Printing Press*. Story after story, piece after piece, he read them. He poured himself a shot after each story, and after he was halfway through his bottle, he spoke.

"GLMT. Give me an optimistic science fiction story on automation. The protagonist is a struggling genius. No one believes him when he tells the world about his alternative approach to automation. Seventy-five thousand words. Use my journalism as research inputs. And some other contemporary authors for voice. Go, go, go!"

The screen flashed green, a blue line sliding across it. Some minutes later, Gautam saw it. He couldn't deny it was his story. It was his voice. No. It was better than his voice, better than anything he would ever compose. He printed it out and leaned back into his chair. Bleary eyed, he drank directly from his bottle, his novel resting like a heavy paperweight on his chest.

Vikram Ramakrishnan is an alumnus of the University of Pennsylvania and enthusiastic member of Odyssey Writing Workshop's class of 2020, where he received the Walter & Kattie Metcalf Scholarship He's the winner of the 17th Annual Gival Short Story Award, and his stories have been published or are forthcoming in *Asimov's Science Fiction, The Year's Top Hard Science Fiction 7*, and *The Chicago Quarterly Review*.

A Blood of Silver Stars

Raymond W Gallacher

T he neighbour's eyes were always on me as I left in the evening. I was tall and striking, makeup understated, well dressed for the neighbourhood. I knew what they thought; what they suspected about me. After all, how could I afford an apartment on my own, even in such a cheap block? How could I afford the nice clothes? Their suspicions were pretty reasonable, their conclusions as good a cover as any. In a neighbourhood full of immigrants and refugees on welfare, they saw my ability to run my tiny two rooms on my own in a poor light.

The truth? I was the best nano drainer in the city. Sex work got you six months; getting caught draining got you at least ten years.

If asked, I was at university and when time allowed, I worked in coffee shops and a Gold Coast harbour brunch spot and took any evening shift I could get. Sometimes I went out with a friend from school. I had given up my studies a year before and I would probably never go back. As for an apartment of my own, that hadn't been the original plan. My father was a refugee whose papers didn't stick. He moved on. Said he was going to get a few things sorted out. *He'd make a good life for us. But there was this deal he'd heard about.* I'd been hearing versions of that for years and was old enough not to give it any credence. Sounds harsh but if immigration didn't get him, then his bookie would. When he left, I didn't even ask where he was going. He'd never been around much anyway. His leaving was just one less thing to worry about.

Out on the landing of that concrete apartment block, I made a play of fussing with my phone and purse, all with a smile on my face. A nice, normal girl going downtown, enjoying her life.

The men – and I mostly chose men – were always in good hotels in the central business district. That's where the *haves* are to be found. My preference was for older business types: they were easier to deal with. I avoided the young and bulky. I'd had a wrist fractured before and learned a hard lesson from it: pick someone you can manage and get it over with.

The first time was tough. Then you get smart. You prepare for the worst. In my purse, I carried a two-shot pistol that Sandor had ghosted for me. It was of a big enough calibre to drop a fair-sized man and small enough to flush down the toilet. I'd never used it. The gun was a last resort. You could forget any notion of jujitsu on the carpet; my bones wouldn't take that. No, I needed a smile, a believable story, the bottle of Allosoporin hidden in my tote, and to move fast.

Not that hotel security had ever given me a second look. My act was too good for that. I was never furtive. In fact, I made a point of being noticed. Just a girl going on a date. A girl who liked a certain type: older, divorced men with first-class medical cover. *Really* good medical cover. That's how you got those silver darlings into your bloodstream.

The atrium of the Pacific Central was busy in that late rush hour kind of way. There were a few early diners in the restaurant and more than a few finishing their business day with cocktails. I stood and waited to be noticed. I'm mixed race, attractive in the right light, and I had learned to be something of a chameleon. I checked my phone and looked around. Just a little nervous, almost shy. In looking so uncomfortable, I looked normal. Pretending you were never in the place is too hard. Modern security is far too smart for that. It's better to have a story that you can't be tripped up on.

Yes, I was at the Pacific Central.

Sorry never seen this man before. Just went to meet a guy. He never showed. I went home. That was all.

The Allosoporin does the rest. It leaves them kind of confused.

I called for him from the desk, and he suggested I come up to his room. I'd contacted him through the *New in Town* website. My face wouldn't exactly be the one on the site, but we wouldn't be together long.

His name was Max and he was one of Sandor's marks. I had to play along with that sometimes. "The real thing," as Sandor had said. "VP of a medical insurance company. That compensation isn't just about money."

When he opened the door, he was neat and well groomed, with thick, silver hair swept back from his forehead and the skin of a younger man. That was a good sign. I looked over his shoulder. It was a suite. That was also a good sign.

"I'm Linda," I said. Then lowered my voice. "We messaged."

His eyes narrowed. I should have been a businesswoman in her mid-fifties, divorced and ready to date again, or at least that was what was on the profile I had uploaded. Max was a little puzzled, but not suspicious. No one likes to have their dating habits discussed in a hallway, so he let me in and closed the door behind us. Whatever he was going to say would remain unspoken.

I made it all very quick. Just pulled the cap off the needle and pressed it into his neck.

Max took a few seconds to react. Surprise rather than anger. I put my arms firmly around him as his legs buckled. He was hauling in air for a scream as I lowered him down to the ground.

"Quiet," I said, putting my hand over his mouth. "You'll live."

When he was out cold, I took the vacuum tubes out of my purse and filled one after the other from his arm. Even unconscious, Max had a healthy glow about him.

I was in no hurry and drew a litre.

"You're quite the catch, Max," I said as I put the vials of blood in my purse. "Hope you meet some nice woman your own age soon."

I opened his airway and left, walked calmly down two flights of stairs, took the elevator down the last flight for the look of it, and strode out to the street, stately and calm.

"Nice job, Linda. You really are my best girl." Sandor treated the vacuum tubes with more anticoagulant, put them into the centrifuge, and turned it on. "Usual deal?"

He got a tight smile from me and not much else. I wasn't Sandor's girl, and I had no intention of ever being one. The usual deal: the percentage – call it what you will – never stayed the same. Sandor always wanted a little more of you. He wanted control, especially over me. The fact that I was clean in every other way made me attractive to him, but hard to leverage. Well, that was his problem. Our relationship was simple. I was a good blood taker, but I needed his lab to process my share. Apart from that, I had no interest in him at all. He was stocky, prone to bad food, and had the skin that came with it. His expression was a permanent smirk. Sandor was a type. The world is full of them. He had an instinct for need and he knew that I needed him. Slowly but surely, he'd been showing his colours over the months I'd been working the hotel game.

His lab was just a lockup out on the hinterlands of the city. It wasn't a high-end operation. He nano-jacked too, but I wasn't interested in that. I wasn't *that* poor. I just wanted some good quality generics extracted from the blood and cleaned, no enhancement. If he'd really had the skill for that, he'd have been doing it for a good salary and not out of a lockup. Sandor reinforced the idea of how much I needed him by overselling his knowledge. I knew his background. He was a nurse who had gotten struck off for dabbling in med tech well beyond his pay grade. You don't get just a written warning for that. Only three companies make med nano. Any hospital that wants their goods play by their rules. And they *do* rule.

I had made two lifestyle mistakes. Being born with bad genetics and going to Sandor to buy my first dose. I had compounded this with letting Sandor set me up with a few marks to cut down the cost of his services. He found these guys by searching a medical database, but he didn't vet them, not as carefully as I would have. The first encounter got me a black eye and a chipped tooth.

After that, I played it my own way.

Meeting through the dating sites was my idea. It was safer, easier to explain away, and more importantly, Sandor didn't know anything about it.

He let his fingers flick over the edge of the centrifuge as it span. "These are generics. Bronze plus."

"Fine with me," I said evenly.

Eighty percent of all nano injections were a general prophylactic. Just tissue repair. Kind of low-key fountain of youth for a thousand a month. They're designed to be broken down by your liver and pissed out after thirty days. Then you get your next shot and swipe your card. Safer for you; good for the company that made them. People like Max and friends could afford to have that done every thirty days. I couldn't.

When the centrifuge slowed and stopped, he decanted the nano layer into saline and reached for a syringe and a needle. True professional that he was, he showed me it came out of a new pack. "You want to do it yourself?"

I shook my head and pulled back the sleeve of my dress, baring my arm. The dose went in and I got to stay out of a wheelchair a little longer.

"Pleasure doing business," he said. "Linda, you don't realise your potential."

Oh Christ. Now the mansplaining. It never took Sandor long before he started the sentence with: *Your problem is...* or *What you need to think about...*

I clamped my jaw shut and tried to look mildly interested.

He picked up one of the other vacuum tubes. "This is okay. Just okay. You could get better than this."

"I don't touch military or off-world. That's twelve years staring at the desert through bars." I rolled my sleeve back down.

"Think about it."

I promised him I would and got out of his lockup and into fresh air as quickly as I could.

Doctor Sue always saw me. She was young, only a few years older than me, small-boned and had skin with that outdoor glow.

She gave my vital signs a quick check, asked me questions about pain, about mobility, about unexpected bruising. I showed her a few bruises. (One which I got from bumping into a table while exiting a hotel at speed.) The occasional discolouration was helpful. It distracted from the fact that I should have been degenerating faster.

"I'm having a good month," I told her.

"Take it when you get it," she said with smiling eyes. There was a shelf behind her. Plush toys and dolls sat all along it. The stuffed little bodies propped themselves up against family pictures. Husband and a kid. A calico cat sitting in a cardboard box. It looked like a nice life.

"You in pain?"

Her question called me back to a reality that was far from hers. "Not acute. Dull throb in lower legs."

She ran her hands over my ankles, then up over my wrists. That's where the small fractures and bruising shows.

"Think we'll keep the prescription going," she said, mostly talking to herself.

It was just painkillers and supplements. They didn't rebuild bone tissue the way the nanos did, but my level of healthcare didn't cover that kind of therapy. I got access to the public health system, but I rated the bare minimum. Acute therapy I could get. Not long term. Private? Not in a million years on my coffee shop wages.

She wrote out the form and filled in the time with some light chat.

You still in school?

You working?

Where?

Oh, I know that spot.

Then, "Let me take a blood sample."

That rocked me. She didn't usually do that.

"Prescription's fine," I said, just a little too sharply.

Sue raised an eyebrow. Puzzled. Not used to hostility, especially from me.

"I need to do blood work, Linda."

I panicked. Simple as that.

I made excuses that I had to go. "I have work."

She didn't argue. But as I got to the door, she said quietly, "Be careful out there."

There were a couple of conventions that following month. They made for good hunting. Sandor sent me a list of suitable targets. I just messaged back, *OK,* then ignored it. I was safer on my own.

I put a lot of well-chosen images and profiles where the rich and available might be interested and selected three that seemed right. Two of them worked for medical companies and would be in town. *Perfect.* It was time to exchange some emails and put in a little groundwork.

Were they in an easily accessed hotel?

Did they have private security?

Were there stairs and a rear door?

All the kinds of things a nicely brought up girl needs to know.

The first week was very fruitful. In fact, I tumbled two very charming men on the same day. Now that's audacity for you.

I took the vacuum tubes back to Sandor's lab and endured his lack of charm and hygiene while he processed them.

"This old geezer: nothing, babe. Maybe he lives a clean life. No booze and a lot of yoga."

"The other guy?"

"Score."

"What are they?"

"Nonspecialised generics." He shrugged. "But they'll do."

I watched him decant, mix, then decant again into a saline solution and then up into a syringe. He fixed the needle and gave me something close to a sympathetic look. If there was one thing I was sick of, it was needles. I had been treated like a pin cushion since I was a teenager.

"I got ideas, Linda."

"I'll bet," I said, staring at the sunlight pinpricking through his tin roof.

"You can collect, no doubt about that. You're my top taker. Now, I have clients looking for top batch. Not Silver. Gold. I've seen their money, Linda. Let's move up in the world."

Right.

"Sandor," I said, slowly and carefully. "I have early onset osteoporosis. Brittle bones. This…" I waved my hand between us. "Is a medical necessity."

"One time, Linda. Soft target."

"No."

Then it came. I knew it would.

"It's a tight market, Linda. We have to help each other. If we don't, we get in each other's way."

That was the first threat. It was low level, but there was no mistaking what was being said. Quickly, I ran through what he had on me. Lists of marks that he sent to my phone for a start. I'd drained a couple of them before I started making my own arrangements. That alone could mean a year in prison for each one. I backpedalled. Bought time.

"Civilian only. Get me some names," I said. "But I decide whether it's go, no go."

As I thought he might, he looked pleased with himself. "Of course, Linda. You're the best on the street. This is the payoff we deserve. Both of us."

He sent me names. All to my device, purposefully incriminating. The addresses were private homes. No chance. Being in a hotel or even a hospital at the wrong place and at the wrong time was something I could explain away. I couldn't talk my way out of being found in somebody's house. Later that day, to stop the walls of my flat closing in on me, I went out, found a quiet coffee shop, sat in the corner, drank espresso up to the point of hallucination and tried to think through what my life had become.

One. Meds. I needed the meds. Brittle bone isn't just degenerative. It hurts. I needed to work and live, and I needed to do it without pain.

Two. Sandor. Replace Sandor? Sure. But I could get myself mixed up with even more of a creep.

Three. Leave the city. An option. But I'd still end up in the hands of another Sandor. If not, in a year I'd be in a wheelchair.

Four. Learn to do my own extractions. Not a better option. That was just another crime with a suitably big sentence.

Five. There was no five. Except that Sandor would start to increase the pressure soon.

Short or long term. I had no solutions.

My next potential relationship pushed all the right buttons. He was a business consultant and travelled three days of the week. Great: that meant I could encourage a hotel meeting. Reece was sixty, but from his picture looked about forty. That's what you call a clue in the leeching game.

I set up my profile and made a whole new Linda, older, wiser and had been single for five years. My messages were as practiced as my online personality. He bit.

How about lunch in your hotel? Girl has to be safe, you know?

What's your room number there?

Will I ask at the desk? That's okay, right?

The Saint Charles was a nice old pile that I had worked about six months before. The vestibule was open, airy, and all Greek pillars and big ferns. It was like walking into the botanic gardens and offered just as much natural cover. Better than that, the back exit was easily found from the basement.

I arrived early on purpose. It was a good excuse to find his room in a fake fluster.

Third floor. Room 12.

At 312, I knocked and waited. He opened the door and gave me the look. That one that said *she is even better than the picture.* Then again, why wouldn't I appear young for my age? He did.

From that moment on, it went downhill.

The very handsome and distinguished Reece, my height, slim and with very fine pepper and salt hair, was both suspicious and just a little smarter than I was. There was also – although I never saw it – a pressure pad in the room because as I followed him in, all bright and bubbly and drawing out the Allosoporin, he must have stepped on it. Maybe he'd been drained before. Maybe he thought it was a good, old-fashioned robbery. I still got the needle into him, but before I lowered him to the ground with his eyes rolling back in his head, he certainly hit something.

Hotel security is never stealthy, even expensive hotel security. I had him propped up on the sofa and the needle hovering above one of his veins when I heard the heavies burst out of the elevator like big, over muscled corks out of a bottle. I didn't think twice, just ran for the door. Fortunately, his suite was close to the stairs. I walked out, calm as you like, turned that corner and ran down to the floor below. They wasted time hammering on salt and pepper's door then, I imagine, making sure he was alive.

Another two floors and I buzzed for the elevator. When the doors closed, sweat beaded on my forehead. My hand was in my purse tight around that little two shot the whole journey down. "Oh Jesus," I breathed. My heart was about to burst through my chest. "There's got to be a better way."

When the elevator opened, I held my head high, walked through the ferns at a fair old clip, then out of the rotating doors like I owned the place. A block further and I ran until I found somewhere backstreet bar to drink until I stopped shaking.

I went to the health centre once a month. No choice. If I didn't keep my appointments, it would look odd; worse, suspicious. That was the last thing I wanted. And at the practical level, if I got struck off the patient list, I couldn't even get painkillers. Usually, I wiggled my appointment time until I was sure that any guests were out of my system. By then, I would bruise more easily and picked up micro fractures like dog hair. It had worked so far. I just had to keep my nerve.

Doctor Sue welcomed me, opened my file, and went through her checks. We chatted about all the standard lightweight stuff.

I'm doing Tai Chi now.

How's that?

I love it. Got to be something in that energy flow, right?

41

We did temperature, pulse. Then the usual questions. Swelling? Fractures? Discolouration? Sue checked my hands and wrists, looking for lumps and bruises. "Some bruising. Not much. In fact, you look good."

She wrote out my prescription out in a nice fine hand. "You sure you're a real doctor?" I asked.

"I hope so." Sue looked up from her pad. "Can I take blood this time?"

I thought about the dates one more time. "Of course," I said. "Sorry about last time. It's needles. I have to prepare myself for them. Like a kid. Stupid, I know."

That got a nice smile, a genuine one. When the smile faded and she returned to her professional face, she asked, "You a refugee?"

"Yes, but I have leave to stay."

"Tough life. Family?"

I shook my head.

"Do you work?" she asked.

"Yes. Just coffee shops. Restaurants."

"Then that's a start. Let's leave the bloods right now. Those labs, they can analyse down to the milligram." She pushed a leaflet towards me. There was a couple on the front, walking down a country lane hand in hand. It was autumn and yellowed. Fallen leaves littered the path, but that didn't bother them or their investment portfolio. Sue tapped the bill with her pen. "This company has a payment plan. They do nanos perfect for your condition. Rebuild your bone at the rate it deteriorates."

I opened the page and looked at the monthly cost. No chance. I couldn't even come close.

"Looks good," I said, all bright eyed but serious.

She finished writing the prescription and pushed it across her desk. I thanked her, picked it up and took the leaflet for effect.

"Linda," Sue said. "Contact them. This is your way out. There are medical charities, maybe reach out to them. But if you're taking something from the street, I can't treat you anymore. I'm sorry but I can't. I have my practice to think about."

I didn't argue and didn't play the innocent. She deserved better than that. "I'll see what I can do," I said. "And thanks. Thanks for your care."

Some traps aren't about money. They're about circumstances.

Blood takers are thieves. I would have to steal all my life just to stay out of a wheelchair. Whether you put yourself in a vulnerable position for cash or for a suspension of med nanos didn't matter. The result was the same. You got caught, you got prison, or you got hurt.

You want to know what you are? You're plastic.

Enough heat and pressure? You'll bend.

Given long enough, you don't even know who you are anymore; you just be what you have to be.

You will put armour around your heart.

You become an opportunist.

One day, you see a way out and you reach for it. Even if there's a chance you could end up worse.

His name was Anthony, and he was both a beginning and an end.

On the outskirts of the city, there was a small Defence Force dock. That crowd was, shall we say, not my market. Those boys and girls, should they want a good time, can find that in any bar or club. Yes, they got med injections as part of service, but they were just generics. Quality Bronze Batch generics but generics none the less. The juice wasn't worth the squeeze. Especially if I was running the risk of getting my soft-boned head bust.

So, in general, what they had, I neither needed nor wanted.

Then there's Off World Defence. That's a small cadre and nothing is too good for them. No jealousy on my part. Who wants to die the way they die?

The med support is the best. Gold plus and more.

Those bugs will repair your torn guts while you lie there on your acceleration couch screaming. They'll repair your bones when they've been turned to powder, and you'll be glad of it even if you never quite walk right for the rest of your life. Oh, they do the job. *Like nothing on Earth.* Also, they don't break down in your liver, at least not in a month. A month is no good off world. They're efficacious for two years from just one injection. A regular hospital doesn't even keep those tiny beads in stock. Anybody who tells you that they can get their hands on that commodity is probably lying and if you buy any of it from them, you're an idiot.

The real stuff is the unicorn, but the price is too high. Stealing it or selling it isn't just everyday crime. It gets you the kind of court that has no jury.

His full name was Anthony Jardine.

A nice name, I thought.

Anthony's name and picture didn't come from Sandor. I found Anthony my way. Late forties, stocky. Wanted to meet new people. He was on a site for older and divorced; all very open and public, not some hook-up pages. I had developed the knack of reading the look of some people. He seemed like a nice guy, good profile, reasonable likes and interests. Sporty but bookish. Good spread of pictures. Anthony on top of mountains. Anthony at the Biennale. Anthony walking on a winter beach.

I tapped the screen and flicked a few more pictures. "Not a bad catch, Anthony," I said. "Pity all I want is your plasma."

I ran his face through every filter and every wanted list. Nothing. I couldn't find a work profile for him either. I should have been wary about that: no point putting him face down on the carpet if he wasn't at least on the Enhanced Silver med package, was there?

My occupation, though, was always slightly reliant on chance.

I created a new profile for myself and made sure it suited him. Aged myself by about twenty years and invented a nice backstory. That Linda had an art gallery, a messy divorce and no kids. I messaged him an introduction and the next day we were chatting back and forth. Funny, the fake dating was something I had developed a talent for, but then, apart from my other problems, I was lonely.

He offered me a lunch date at the Montgomery, and I gladly accepted while topping up the Allosoporin.

The Montgomery was a new venue to me, and an unwelcome discovery. I had expected a hotel or a club. Instead, the block was managed apartments. They were very exclusive, had a small reception area, and seemed designed for security and discretion. The restaurant was an attached building next door. *No. Just no.* It wasn't right for me. I turned to go.

"Help you, miss?"

He had come out of the office without a sound. Neat, turtleshell glasses, understated suit. I was caught off guard and stumbled a little. "I'm meeting someone. Might be in the wrong place." I put my phone back in my purse and had every intention of exiting straight out of the Montgomery that moment, but he asked, "Apartment?"

"Menteith."

"Ah, Mr Jardine. Let me buzz you through."

If I'd turned and ran, it would have been suspicious. It was best to be the person I was supposed to be. The elevator opened with hardly a sound, and I stepped in.

Seeing Anthony in the flesh was all the confirmation I needed that I had made a mistake.

He looked like he'd had more than a few rejuvenation treatments and some good care. His build was heavy, but he moved easily, like a much younger man. He introduced himself and welcomed me in. Whatever else he said was lost on me when we shook hands, because those hands just didn't feel right. Skin on steel.

I should have faked my way out of that door right then, but I kept going. That, I suppose, was my problem. I had learned to be a little too self-reliant.

Inside, the place was great. Split level with a screened bedroom and a small galley kitchen. I could have moved in myself.

His luggage was near the bed.

There was a suit in a dry-cleaning cover. Under the cover was a midnight blue uniform, a sun on the upper arm. Add that to the look of him, to the feel of his hands. He was Off World. Of course he was. I couldn't even blame Sandor for this set up. I'd picked him myself.

"Drink?"

"What?" I was stunned for a second. "Sure, thanks." We were supposed to be meeting for a date, I thought. *Pull yourself together.*

"Are you all right?"

He had a nice voice. Mellow. Kind.

I was panicking, and it must have shown.

"Is there anything else you want to tell me? Or was your rejuv just really good?"

Usually, I never allowed the interaction to get to that stage. He should have been face down by this time.

"Gin and tonic."

"Sure," he said, still giving me a leery eye.

If his problem was anything, it was over confidence. When these types are groundside, they feel invincible. He gave me a smile and turned to open a little bar. "Better tell me the whole story. Whatever your name is."

I don't think Anthony suspected me as a blood leech, but it didn't matter. Kind voice or not, the drugs in my purse would get me prison time. My choices were poor. There were no back stairs to take. If he decided to hold me in that room, there wouldn't be much I could do about it. I'd felt the power in those hands. Sometimes it doesn't matter if the decision you make is good or bad, as long as you make a decision.

I reached into my purse, drew out the Allosoporin and stuck the needle into his neck. His elbow went into my gut, and I slumped to my knees, but the dose was in.

Anthony did not go down easily. Even throwing my body weight on him didn't change much. He was strong, not just physically and with a lot of enhancement. He was mentally strong. No, he did not give up his consciousness without a struggle. I held on to him in a chokehold as he thrashed around. Another dose of Allosoporin might have done it but my bag was out of reach on the floor. I prayed to God through clenched teeth, *Get me out of this one and I'll believe in you again.*

He drew in huge gulps of air, trying to keep control over himself. No way was the Allosoporin going to hold this boy down for long. When he finally settled, I turned his head so he could breathe. The idea of draining him never even crossed my mind. All I wanted was out.

I stood up, tried to slow my breathing down.

Leave nothing behind.

I grabbed my bag and made sure everything was in it. Prints? No, didn't touch the glass. DNA? Probably. Too bad. I ran to the mirror and fixed myself up. Anthony was coming round already. By my rough estimate, he was processing the drugs four times faster than anyone I'd come across before.

There was a small black case near his luggage. It had that medical symbol on it, the snake around a staff. I never stole, neither physical goods nor money, but partly out of curiosity, I grabbed for it and broke it open. Inside was his carry-on med kit. Trauma on one side and, yes, eight tiny vials on the other.

Gold. Eight vials of Gold.

I took three and made for the door.

Anthony was almost on his feet, but I stopped and turned back into the room again.

There was Montgomery Apartments notepaper on it on a bureau, one of those fake writing tables you get in every hotel. I picked up a pen and pad and scribbled down: *I'm sorry. I'm really sick.*

I made myself look respectable in the elevator mirror and was almost my normal self by the time I stepped out into reception. Walking straight wasn't easy. I had a fractured shoulder, for sure.

Turtleshell glasses gave me an enquiring glance.

"So glad I kept my nerve," I said. "Now *that* man has potential."

I put two of the suspensions into ordinary vacuum tubes, along with some blood from the butchers. Then I gave them to Sandor and told him I didn't need a dose for another two weeks, but I'd be back.

At the end of the block, I made an anonymous phone call to the cops. He'd do ten years in high security for those silver darlings and that was fine with me. To use his own words: *we got in each other's way.*

I hated needles, but at home I took a deep breath and shot one of those gold star suspensions straight into my veins. "You have eight months on this dose alone, Linda," I said to myself. "Use it."

I bought a ticket south. On a good old fashioned road bus, can you believe that? I had a notion for somewhere cooler and quieter. Away from Defence Security and away from some cop who took a genuine interest in their job. Away from the trade. Away from anyone who ever saw me or might recognise me.

I estimated I had a year and a half to make myself into a new person. New look, good job, and a health plan. I'd ride on a wave of those silver darlings.

I changed before. I could change again.

Raymond W Gallacher is based in Glasgow and writes science fiction by night and business tech during the day. Raymond returned to education after a life changing event and studied The Novel and Short Story at Glasgow University. He is always working on his next story or that hoped for novel.

Soulmark

Brandon Crilly

I **'m used to hearing people** over cheers and drum solos, but the woman with the dragonfly wings throws me for a second.

"You wanna *what?*"

"To. Dazzle. Him." The woman stretches, showing off the glitter on her bare neck and arms. People lean away from her translucent wings – definitely not a prop, like I thought when they were folded behind her Garrison and the Matchsticks T-shirt.

Great. Instead of using magic wings to, I don't know, rescue people from forest fires – if they're that functional – she thinks they'll earn a backstage pass.

I pitch my voice over the audience as the Matchsticks finish a song. "Lee's not interested. And you *aren't*. Crossing. This." I point at the metal railing separating the amphitheater seats from the pit.

Dragonfly Lady sways in place for a minute, either surprised by my response or … no, something else, the way her cheeks flush under the glitter.

"*Vicky, you good?*"

My hand stops halfway to my earpiece when those wings flex again. If Dragonfly Lady got her soul's worth from her Deal, the Molson Seventy-Sixth might be trending tonight. She should've been turned away at the door, but now she's my problem.

Snapping my fingers catches her attention. My hand drifts down to the railing, grips it and crushes it like putty. That sobers her up. She looks for a Soulmark, maybe realizing for the first time that not everyone who makes a Deal is as obvious about it. That's why I wear a high collar.

All I do is smirk. Dragonfly Lady withers, wings folding down and she steps into the crowd.

On the stage behind me, the Matchsticks launch into "Wayward and Lonesome." I grit my teeth and almost put another dent in the railing, since that song is *not* supposed to be in tonight's setlist. Apparently, I'm doomed to live out my last days being proven right all the time.

I gesture for in-house security to take my place. Halfway to the stage, Horatio blasts my ear: "*Fucksake, he's going into the crowd again.*"

Of course, I already know that, but Lee's manager is usually a step behind. Being the Matchsticks' security head means acting quick to avert disaster. Like some drunk, winged fangirl flying onto the stage. Or Lee being a dumbass.

The fans singing along to "Lonesome" ignore me marching between the stands and the pit. They've only got eyes for Lee Garrison ambling down the thrust stage, one hand raised like a Baptist preacher in leather and denim. The pit audience can't reach him; security checks for all sorts of wacky stuff at the door these days, ever since that idiot with the extendable arms at the Fistful of Awesome show. They wave and cheer and Lee continues unharmed, toward where the thrust stage meets Area

Three.

People don't see the other side of a concert. I get it. Between the sound, the lights, and the energy, you get lost in a live show. That's your right, since you've paid for the escape. Or you're watching a YouTube video like, "Girl Dances on Stage with Springsteen" and wishing you were the one holding hands with a rock star.

Live shows aren't magical for us. The Molson Seventy-Sixth holds seventeen thousand people, each of them a potential problem. I'm not even talking about someone sneaking a Soulmark, a knife or some coke inside. Maybe that girl at Springsteen's show trips and takes The Boss down with her. Or one of the lovely, excited fans reaching from the front row pokes Lee in the eye by mistake and destroys his cornea.

Or he almost breaks his neck going into the crowd. Again.

Taking the crew stairs two at a time brings me to Area Three as Lee hops off the stage, three steps from the stands. Corina and Tomas flank him as he belts out the chorus to "Lonesome." The fans scream even louder when he starts shaking hands and giving high-fives. No one's bothered by the sweat dripping from his tousled brown hair or staining the front of his shirt. A messy god is still a god.

Lee climbs the railing for the final chorus and the audience grabs at him.

I get there first, clenching his leather jacket. Corina and Tomas watch the crowd, knowing that Lee isn't going anywhere now. Except back upstage, when he's finished.

While "Lonesome" fades, Lee's stare is intense. I think he's spotted something I won't like, but nothing catches my eye in the crowd. For a half-second, he looks … disappointed, I think.

He's all smiles again when he drops from the railing, probably landing too hard on his knees. I give him my shoulder as he climbs back onstage.

The thing is, Lee Garrison is just a guy. Everything special about him is genuine, which is part of why he's still popular, twenty years and thirteen albums into his career. Unlike too many younger musicians these days, Lee's ability didn't come from a Deal.

Luckily for him, mine did.

After every show, Lee slams two glasses of water backstage, shares congratulations with the band and spends a ten-minute decompression in whatever green room the venue sets aside. For some rockers that means blow or conjuring iguanas or whatever, but for Lee it's truly a moment to come down from the high of doing what he loves.

I don't give him that moment tonight.

Hazem is on door duty; he steps aside without a word and opens it for me. Lee's facing the mirror at the back, in a fresh T-shirt, hastily wiping tears from his eyes.

That throws me more than Dragonfly Lady, even though I've seen the man shirtless, upside down in a chocolate fountain or in a dozen other embarrassing moments before he got sober. I start examining the furniture, mostly two old leather sofas the Seventy-Sixth probably brought in for tonight.

"Sorry, Vic, something in my eye." The tears are gone when Lee turns to face me. "What's up?"

Since I don't have much imagination, I tell him, "I came here to scold you."

Lee looks confused for a second, until his face lights up and he starts to laugh. He plops down on a sofa. "Okay. Lay into me, Vic."

Somehow this lanky, middle-aged man-child reminds me of Carter whenever I caught him on YouTube instead of doing homework.

Now I'm the one looking away.

Lee shifts. "I didn't actually worry you, did I?"

I shake off the memory and frown at him. "You're supposed to stay onstage. If Horatio didn't have a stroke, he's on his way down."

"I figure."

"That's four – wait, five shows in a row, Lee. Rule was that you stay onstage for half of the shows, until your doctor clears you."

"Disappointed you, didn't I?" he says, offering a grin.

"Yeah." I try to make it clear with one word how serious I am. I don't have the time for him to bullshit and not take care of himself. Especially since he won't have me forever.

Lee scratches the side of his head. "Look, I'm sorry. Shouldn't have gone out there." I figure that's it, but he adds something that doesn't sound like Lee: "No excuse, either. Being selfish."

Garrison and the Matchsticks perform almost year-round, sometimes as many as eighteen shows a month, only breaking to record albums or when someone has a baby. Why? No joke, it's because of the fans. Lee'll do any charity invite he can, small venues or large, sign memorabilia or take a selfie, and even insists on a certain percentage of every show's profits going to local charities. He said to me once, *I love music, but the fans love the show. And they matter more.*

Thinking back to that expression on his face earlier, I ask: "What were you looking for tonight?"

He rolls his shoulders. While I wait him out, I hear Tomas in my earpiece: "*Management inbound, capitana.*"

"Balls."

Lee smirks. "Horatio?" He leans forward, hands clasped together over his knees. "You ever regret taking your Deal?"

For a second, I feel Sinister Shad's hand tracing the Soulmark on my neck. No one asks me about it anymore; they know the basics, Horatio and the execs know when my time is up, and that's enough for everyone.

"Every day," I say. Carter is almost sixteen now. Gillian must be freaking about him driving.

Lee's bushy eyebrows rise.

"Don't tell me you're thinking of taking one."

"Shit no. Just things on my mind, got me curious." He lays back against the sofa. "Looking for a face. In the audience. She wasn't there tonight, so never mind."

I want to ask him who, but the door slams open and Horatio starts roaring. By the time he's done, we're overdue getting Lee on the bus, and I have more pressing things to worry about than his questions and tears.

We hit Burlington on Friday and check-in at the Delta. The Matchsticks have sold-out shows Saturday and Sunday. In between, I'm off-duty and head to my local downtown haunt: Kempling's, attached to a brewery and named after some dead MP. The music is low, only half the polished oak tables are ever full, and the place's theme has nothing to do with the Bible.

I've never understood why the whole "angels and demons" fad never faded. The beings going around granting Soulmarks aren't demons; I remember a Dealer saying on TV once that it's sort of offensive. That year, something like four separate movies popped up about good demons facing prejudice.

You can't escape them completely, though. Every now and then the flatscreens show a commercial for a Dealmaker firm. The news talks about some well-known Canadian whose clock ran out recently. Tonight, they're repeating a story about the latest Timeout who recorded his last day. They all do that, giving instructions on adding sepia or certain cuts for a final music video, sometimes even setting up the "perfect" moment to drop lifeless to the floor. There are so many Timeouts now that Tomas and the crew's other young folks admit they can't keep track.

But yeah, those sorts of reminders are everywhere, so they don't bother me.

I don't like when a Dealer walks into Kempling's, though.

Most wear all black, which doesn't help their image much; Sinister Shad told me they can see black "more clearly," but mostly the government-mandated red pin stands out more on dark clothes. This one looks almost middle-aged, round-faced and vaguely Caucasian, but stooped like someone twice as old. The redness around his eyes stands out more than most Dealers, and his lips are pulled back more, showing off a grin filled with way more teeth than necessary. Part of me wishes the Secrecy Act hadn't forced the Dealers to stop masquerading as humans; their attempt to make it clear they aren't is too freaky sometimes.

My regular haunts are where Dealers don't show up. Something's changed at Kempling's; there's a drink waiting at the end of the bar. The Dealer doesn't leer or lean into anyone's personal space as he goes to collect it. Anyone who meets his eye gets a polite nod, as he sorts the curious from the potential clients.

The Dealer's grin widens when he spots me. Sometimes they like to talk to Soulmarked; supposedly there's a black market for negotiating or transferring souls, against the Dealers' own rules. I focus on the nearest flatscreen.

That's the only reason I see the news before the bar gets loud.

GARRISON SOUL-ED? ROCKER MADE DEAL, SOURCE SAYS.

In the image behind the reporter, Lee's wearing gray denim and that genuine smile, hands spread like someone trying to emphasize his honesty.

A wet hooting sound, like an owl being drowned, hits my right ear. It's the Dealer, wide mouth open as he laughs.

The sound chases me out the front door.

There's a lot of fuss through the night.

None of us can get near Lee. Corina says Horatio stormed into his room; an hour later he hasn't left. They're likely Zooming studio execs and lawyers, hopefully only strategizing how to deal with tabloid lies and clickbait.

Hope doesn't keep me from spending the next hour smashing wheel stops in a back-alley parking lot. When I get tired of that I light up my first cigarette in years and wander back.

Lots of people take Deals. I did, for crying out loud, so I'm not one to judge.

I turn a corner and see the Delta down the street, a gang of reporters loitering out front, and a figure with dragonfly wings two meters ahead of me.

Tears glisten against the sparkles on her cheeks. A while ago that might have gotten to me – if she's less angry these days, Gillian can vouch that I have a thing for cheering up pretty girls – but this time alarm bells ring in my head.

I circle Dragonfly Lady carefully; this wouldn't be the first time a crazed fan tracked Lee down. I take a good look at her eyes, but thankfully she looks stone cold sober.

"It isn't true, is it?"

I step between her and the Delta, fully realizing that if she goes airborne, I'm useless. "You're asking the wrong person."

"You must know him." She's wearing a simple gray tank and khakis now, which almost makes that permanent glitter more striking. Without makeup, I realize she's closer to my age, maybe further into her forties. "Do you think he would do it? Keep it a secret, somehow?"

Between the fourth and fifth wheel stop, I realized that if anyone could keep a Soulmark secret, it wouldn't be Lee. Some rich CEO or the Pope, maybe, but a middle-aged guitar geek who can't work a smartphone? Yeah, right.

Except my half-smoked cigarette says I'm not convinced, and the last thing I feel like doing is comforting someone who gave me trouble. "Why'd you follow us?"

Dragonfly Lady stares at the Delta. "To see him again."

I can't remember what she said at the show. Shine for him? Tonight is not the night.

"Get lost. Lee has enough to worry about." I'm normally more polite, but I can barely keep my voice level. "I see you again, I call the police."

"You're right. I shouldn't have come." A fresh tear rolls down her cheek.

I half-expect her to fly away, but she walks around the same corner I came from. That's slightly disappointing.

Ducking around the reporters isn't hard; sometimes the disappearing act of being a woman over forty who's built like a linebacker has its advantages. Hazem's squeezed into a chair in the front lobby, watching the jackals over his coffee. I take the stairs, hoping seven flights will help me relax.

On the sixth-floor landing, I spot blue jeans and leather boots through the steps.

Lee huffs out a breath, hanging his head as he shuffles to the side so I can pass.

I sit beside him. "Horatio scream himself into a coma yet?"

"Talking to the execs."

We're there for a while before I realize he's staring at my Soulmark.

"You said you regret it?"

If Gillian is still as angry as when she kicked me out, she'd say I don't know how to leave well enough alone.

I ask, "Do you?"

"I might someday."

Nothing breaks inside me. I don't want to throttle him or chew him out, remind him about the people who built their lives around his long career, unlike some Timeout. I'm not angry at Lee. I'm angry about him falling into the same trap I did.

He leans his elbows on the step behind him and grunts. "C'mon, Vic. If anyone can quiz me or give me hell, it's you."

I point at my neck. "Because of this?"

"Because you've been with me longer than almost anyone, time off included. Longest relationship I've ever had with a woman."

I'm honestly not sure I want to know the details. "Any idea how the world found out?"

"Used to be less cameras here."

He takes his elbows off the stairs and rolls up his left sleeve. His hoodie has the vintage art from the Matchsticks' second album, the cathedral made of matches halfway burned to cinders. The dark swirls of the Soulmark on his forearm aren't the same as mine, but supposedly every mark is unique; something to do with souls that no Dealer has ever fully explained, as far as I know.

The mark looks as faded as the hoodie's design. But that doesn't mean anything.

Lee was wearing a T-shirt when I talked to him at the Molson.

"Figured an alley behind a pub would be a safe bet these days. Who knew?"

Part of me wants to call Corina and Hazem and find out how Lee snuck out of the Delta. Knowing the team, though, they allowed it. The band and crew all trust each other. Lee's the one who broke that trust.

I remember the intense look on his face at the Molson, and the tears he hid when I came to the green room. Each explanation that comes to mind is worse than the last.

Lee shrugs. "It's going to sound like a bullshit reason next to yours."

Maybe. At the time my Deal made sense. Sitting with Gillian in the ICU, everyone terrified to go home even knowing the men who broke in had been arrested, I almost went *Death Wish* instead. But trading my soul for the power to protect my family didn't ruin my life. Paranoia and fear did that, along with going behind Gillian's back.

"Been looking for a ghost." Lee sounds wistful. "Did you watch any of the comeback tour in '11?" That was halfway through my break from touring. "First night in Ottawa, I'm leaning over the stage during 'Shield Me' and I see this ... breathtaking woman. The most beautiful smile I've ever seen. Genuine, you know?"

Any other day, his word choice would've made me laugh.

"Almost screwed up my chords. Stupid." Lee shrugs. "Finished the rest of the set. The encore. Then I'm in the green room, and it hits me. I'll never see her again."

His eyes light up with wonder. "Except I did."

He tells me how he went wandering after the show. How he wasn't looking up and almost bumped into this woman. They stepped over each other's words like a bad romcom, he blurted out something about coffee, she made a joke about rock stars always getting what they want, and they found a rare twenty-four-hour Tim Horton's.

"Jolene," he says wistfully. "Laughed three times at that."

They chatted almost until sunrise. Lee offered to escort her home, realized how that sounded and apologized. She said she wasn't from Ottawa, anyway, and staying with friends. But she wrote down her number, since he didn't have a cellphone then.

"What happened?"

"Horatio sent a bunch of my wardrobe to be cleaned. Her number was still in my pocket."

"And?" When he shrugs, it's my turn to give him a look. "You know how easy it is to find people online, right?"

"You don't think I tried? Why do you think I called her a ghost?" Lee throws up his hands. "Shit, I wrote 'Black Coffee' and 'I Won't Walk You Home' about that night. I've tried to call out to her on stage half-a-dozen ways. Too worried about, I don't know, scaring her off or the media going after her. Just hoped she'd come back to a show someday. If I spotted her once…"

I don't want to count how many shows he's played since 2011. "But you haven't."

"Obviously." He idly scratches his forearm, not that the Soulmark itches. "Figure I screwed up my chance, but to see her again … Told you it's stupid."

I remember when people had all sorts of crazy ideas about what a Deal could get done, before the government and Dealers worked out the Secrecy Act. Whatever was discussed keeps them from handing out things like assassinations, brainwashing, or cash deals that would totally screw up the economy. Too bad for Lee, the Act means a Dealer can't conjure someone's SIN or home address, either.

"It promised she can be found."

"Please tell me it gave you more than that."

Lee shrugs. "It's gonna make sure we cross paths. Anything more would feel slimy."

"And what's your end of the Deal?" I ask, not really wanting to know how many years Lee has left. Or months, like me.

Luckily, he replies, "That one stays with me, Vic. Not even the execs get to know."

"Bet they didn't like that."

"Nope." He smirks. "If they were worried, they should've written it into my contract."

The execs debate whether to cancel Lee's shows. No photos online yet proving he's a Soulmarked, which means they can deny it. I spend a lot of time in the Delta's lobby, making eye contact with reporters until they feel awkward. Eventually they move on, probably because another Timeout is about to croak.

When my phone buzzes I expect it's Corina with news. Instead it's from a number I don't recognize: *Mom? It's Carter.*

A second message arrives while I'm frozen: *Mom gave me your number. Are you okay? Call me??*

I couldn't tell you how long I stand there. Gillian's had my number since I rejoined the Matchsticks, in case of emergency, but she's never used it. I thought she deleted it.

The next message I get is Corina, telling me the show is still on. That means I have work to do: scheduling and route-planning and threat assessment and a half-dozen other things that have nothing to do with considering how to respond to my son.

Guess how I spend the next hour.

When Corina finds me later and says the execs changed their mind and postponed the show, I'm grateful for something else to rage about.

Horatio's quiet when I see him. He shows me what's trending: a picture of a nondescript alleyway, which I know is Burlington because Lee is wearing the same clothes as Friday. He's talking with a Dealer I recognize.

Horatio is smart enough not to hand me his phone. I crush my work tablet instead.

If Gillian is willing to give Carter my phone number, she probably remembers that I think sometimes before I react. Security means acting on instinct, not impulse.

My impulse is to find that Dealer from Kempling's and use my Deal-given talents on it. The instinct behind that is obvious, so I take my time and think.

Eventually, I make a phone call. It isn't to Carter, but I don't want my first message to him in years to be fueled by dread and rage. Or risk talking myself out of what I want to do next.

Dealers have routines. At almost the exact same time as the night before, the same Dealer walks into Kempling's, casting the same broken smile. The same drink is waiting at the bar.

I take the stool beside him. "I'd like to chat."

Those red-rimmed eyes clock my Soulmark. His words come out with a prominent slur, one of many tells that Dealers aren't built like humans underneath. "Deals cannot be unmade."

"About something else."

The Dealer sips his drink, which looks like a Caesar except with a curling straw and a powerful reek of cinnamon. "Knowledge that is public?"

"Not quite."

My eyes flick to one of the flatscreens, where a reporter is gearing up for "BUSA Comments on Garrison Deal." Typical trash. The Bureau of Supernatural Arrangements won't talk about the filing they have on Lee's Deal.

The Dealer looks, too, the movement too loose in the neck, and his smile stretches so wide I'm concerned his ears are going to meet behind his head.

"No fan. You are a crafter of news, trying for a scoop?" He draws the last word out slowly, as though it's unfamiliar. "With soulstuff to offer, we might trade, but..." His loose shrug reminds me of an octopus. "Certain things cannot be spoken, even to a Soulmarked."

"Maybe I'm not your average Soulmarked."

The Dealer cocks his head, clearly not understanding. To be fair, I'm not entirely sure if I know what I'm doing. I keep telling myself this isn't the same as when I took my Deal. Probably because I have less to lose, with the clock ticking faster in my head.

"A friend. I understand." The Dealer clicks his uneven teeth. "What would you say to the holder of his soul?" As he lifts the drink again, I get the feeling he's trying to be cool and nonchalant, like he's seen too many movies.

I lean in close to whisper, giving the Dealer a pointed look. "We both know there are ways to transmit a soul," I say, careful with my phrasing. "Just need to make sure no one's watching."

He throws a theatrical glance over his shoulder, as though anyone would be eavesdropping, and swoops his head in toward me. I get a powerful whiff of cinnamon and tomato juice.

Gillian asked me in the ICU if I had lost my mind, wandering into a Dealer firm to sell myself. I remember how angry I felt, hearing her say that through bruised lips. Telling myself she would understand *why* eventually, and everything would be fine.

I wonder what she'd think of this plan.

The Dealer studies me for about twelve seconds. They have ways of figuring out intent; something halfway between telepathy and body language. My intent is clear: I want a private meeting to discuss the black market. Once he sees that, he finishes his drink with one long slurp and beckons me away. We pass a couple servers who don't bat an eye at our presence in the back. I understand why when we hit a tiny room mostly dedicated to shelves and crates, with a wooden table and two chairs in the center.

"Discreet methods are available to the adventurous and needy," the Dealer says as he sits facing the door. "We may discuss terms here."

"You understand what I'm asking?"

"Soulmarks lack permanence, with the right maneuvering."

I take the other seat. "And you'll do it?"

"I can. Carefully." The Dealer waves his hand back and forth. "He who has your soulstuff is not to be easily trifled. What do you offer?"

Someone *tsks* behind me.

The Dealer's not-quite-human eyes go wide as he looks over my shoulder. When I grab his outstretched hand and slam it against the table, there's a loud crack of wood, but the Dealer doesn't make a noise. He tries to wriggle out of my grip, but there's no teleporting or turning into a four-armed grizzly or something. I was told there wouldn't be.

I glance behind me, since I don't completely trust Sinister Shad. The Dealer who owns my soul looks exactly like he did when I met him: in a long black peacoat and three-piece suit like some period gentleman, if that gentleman clearly wasn't human.

"You heard enough?"

"Soulmarks lack permanence? Unfortunate to have said." Shad's *tsking* is wet and disturbing. "Taking soulstuff is guaranteed punishment for trying to skirt our laws. We cannot lie, but some of us enjoy scheming."

I turn back to the other Dealer. Slowly, like in the movies.

"Understand the spot you're in? Nod, please."

He does, stiff as a human would.

"Okay, Morningstar, I want information. Where do I find the woman Lee Garrison is looking for?"

"That is for the client—"

I squeeze hard enough to shatter a human hand. Pieces move around under the Dealer's skin and his teeth slam together. At least I've made us both uncomfortable.

"My obligation is to bring them together."

"Did you agree on bringing them together a certain way, or within a certain time?" Right away I can tell he didn't. "Then let's say I'm your means. Come up with whatever cosmic explanation you want. Lee's not waiting years for this."

"You do not know the full terms of his Deal."

"I know what Lee wants, and I know he deserves better than waiting around for you. Cough it up, or we'll see how far I can go before someone overhears and decides they care."

The Dealer looks at Shad, which is ballsy after trying to steal Shad's property. For a moment, I don't think he's going to tell me, and I'm going to waste some of my precious time in a jail cell after finding out if Dealers scream when they're in pain.

Luckily for us both, he makes the smart choice.

When we leave the room, Sinister Shad says, "Surprising you didn't try to get more from this day."

I consider defending humanity, since not everyone thinks the way Dealers do, but that would make me a hypocrite. "Any chance the Deal gets revoked?"

"If my colleague is punished, it may be possible to prove he took advantage of your Garrison. Time will be needed."

I didn't expect more than that. Not wanting to be impolite, I give Shad a proper nod and start making my exit.

"Thank you for your valuable time, Vicky," Shad says. He learned a smirk at some point, which I like about as much as anything else on a Dealer's face "I look forward to a ... faster reunion."

If Gillian's still upset about losing me, this probably won't help. When you're already counting months, though, a few weeks doesn't feel like a loss. I might owe a Dealer my soul, but I owe Lee my life.

"See you when I see you, Shad," I say, and resist the urge to scratch my Soulmark.

"*Vicky, your guest is at the gate.*"

The brick walls around me thump with a different energy than the Molson. The fans are waiting to see whether Lee pretends like everything is fine or the entire show tanks. Hopefully, they feel lucky the show only got postponed instead of outright cancelled.

I know why I'm nervous, and for once it has nothing to do with security.

The Brant Street Hall doubled their staff tonight, filling the place with yellow-shirted strangers. The last thing I want is my own audience, which is why I chose the smallest, most out-of-the-way gate in the venue. Hazem is there, and he gestures at someone standing behind a pillar. I try not to tense.

Jolene is a cross between the first and second times I saw her, in jeans and a V-neck but with makeup like at the Molson. Her wings tremble against her shoulders.

"You okay? Let's get you inside?" I don't see a convenient spot to place my hand between her wings, so I guide her from afar, worried she might fly away this time. "Sorry for being so gruff before." I've said that to her three or four times now.

"I'm not sure this is a good idea," Jolene says as we walk down the empty corridor. "You said on the phone—"

"That Lee wants to see you." I stop. "If you're not ready, say so. We can turn around."

She shakes her head. "No, I've been wanting this for a long time, too."

I ask her about that night with Lee while we walk. By the time we reach the green room, Jolene's wings have calmed down. She asks me to go in alone first.

Lee's pacing the dirty blue rug, running his hands through his hair. When he turns, even though it's only me, I swear he goes pale like in an old *Casper* cartoon.

"Fuck me."

"Not my job." I beckon at the man-child. "Come on, Lee."

"Thought it'd take some time to find her. Or that you wouldn't even be able to … do I even want to know how?"

"We both have other things to do, Lee."

"Just gimme a damn minute…"

"Lee?" a voice says behind me.

When he sees Jolene in the doorway, Lee's mouth drops open. She starts to back out of the room, but he reaches toward her, catching himself as though he's worried about scaring her off. It's pretty adorable.

Lee's silent for long enough that I feel like smacking him.

Jolene takes his hand. "'Sitting here at this table, coffee cup trembling. Wish I could stop the sunrise from coming. Take my hand, baby, and laugh again…'"

"'So I remember what it sounds like tomorrow.'" Lee grins, finishing the opening to "Black Coffee."

I may have broken that table in half when the Dealer identified Lee's mystery woman. Whether it's bad luck or Lee being taken advantage of doesn't matter, I suppose. Every Deal is partly unfair.

Seeing Lee and Jolene together, I try not to think about the unfair sides. They'll use the time they have wisely.

I close the door behind me and tell everyone Lee will be backstage soon. The rumbling of the audience is faint as I open Carter's latest message: *I hope Lee's okay, he's cool. Talk after?*

He knows the full story of my first Deal. I don't know how he'll react to what I've done now. But I'm not wasting soulstuff on worrying.

Fingers shaking like Jolene's wings, I call my son.

'Soulmark' originally appeared in *Fusion Fragment #7*.

Brandon Crilly's IPPY Award-winning fantasy novel *Catalyst* was published in 2022, followed shortly after by his bestselling games publication, *Bestiarium Vocabulum*. He's also an Aurora Award-winning podcaster, conference organizer for Can*Con, and regularly has too many D&D campaign ideas than he could ever fit into his schedule. Find out more about his upcoming releases by following him on Instagram or signing up for his newsletter via brandoncrilly.com.

SF CALEDONIA

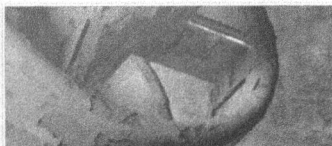

SF CALEDONIA

About   News   Stories   Send us your story   Become a subscriber   Contact

All the stories (so far...)

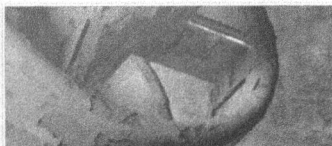

A Cure For Homesickness
Anne Charnock

She retraces her walking commute through the platform's labyrinth. A dose of daylight might help, she thinks, but there's no chance of that. At the end of her fifteen-hour shift at 2700 hours she'll catch the last sunrays out on the viewing . . .

Pussycat, Pussycat
C J Henderson

My new lover has a cat, which, he says, hates everyone but him. I am warned not to go near her—she bites and scratches. I just smile... . . .

The Chrysalis
Laura Scotland

Edith drifted in and out of sleep. She was curled up on the old leather sofa, enjoying the warm, delicate weight of the baby on her chest. . . .

The Worshipful Company Of Milliners
T L Huchu

Every writer wears a hat. Most people may not see it, but it's there, a kind of halo which can be seen if you look from just the right angle. . . .

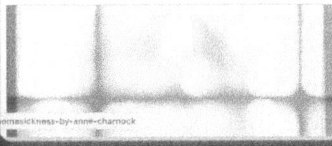

Pssst.... Want to read stories from the best of Scottish SF writers?

For free?

SF Caledonia - the showcase of Scottish Science Fiction is now live.

Stories published regularly

www.sfcaledonia.scot

Cozack and Wallie Got the Zoomies!

Marc A. Criley

The caramel-brown streak of a dog snapped at the heels of the spider-like *maratus* bounding across the field. Ahead, the low hanging branches of a spin oak offered leafy safe harbor and an opportunity. The spindly maratus, larger but lighter than its pursuer, leapt onto the trunk, scurried up to a stout, horizontal branch and scuttled along it. Tracking its quarry, the dog restively paced below, awaited a misstep — its two brown eyes locked onto the ten black unblinking orbs of the clinging beast.

Without warning the maratus spread its fangs and dove onto its target. The dog violently shook and twisted as it raced out from under the tree. Barking, spinning, counter-spinning — it dislodged the attacker, sending it rolling and skidding across the grass. Freed of its burden the dog accelerated flat out across the no-leash park while the maratus flipped back onto its legs and charged off in hot pursuit.

"Cozack and Wallie are so *adorable* when they get the zoomies!" Amongst the diminutive arthropan native's clicks, hisses, and whistles I picked out Penthrex's breathy *zoomies* even without my translator. "Tires me out just watching them."

The two animals raced in a big circle, one of them either dropping back, or the other gaining, until it was hard to tell who was chasing who. It was a warm and beautiful late spring day. Perfect for zoomies. Beta Hydri sunset was a few minutes away, while the system's distant companion star neared high noon. Hours of gorgeous twilight lay ahead, with the city hiveline soon to be twinkling against an azure sky. We sat on one of the picnic tables distributed around the perimeter of the park; me on the bench, Penthrex up on the table itself.

Cozack and Wallie cut the circle and full speed charged one another. They skidded to a halt, nose to chelicerae. Cozack crouched down, fanned out her abdominal flaps. While the aerodynamic braking value was doubtful, the aesthetic effect of the shivering peacock bands of ruby, sapphire, burnt orange, and indigo took one's breath away. She rhythmically slammed her hind legs on the turf, the thumping carrying across the field. Wallie splayed motionless, paws out, growling, butt up, eyes gleaming, metronomic white-tipped tail marking time to Cozack's beat. They would face off this way until one lunged for the other.

"Watch Wallie's tail," I said.

Without breaking their multi-faceted gaze on the standoff, Penthrex rolled a *question ripple* up an antenna. "What about it?"

"Just watch."

71

The faceoff continued, Cozack shivering and flicking her flaps as Wallie yipped short sharp barks. The tail stopped mid-swing, pointing straight up. "There!" I said. Wallie went for one of Cozack's front legs. The maratus may have picked up on the tailsign though; she jerked the leg back, leapt over Wallie's lunge, and tore off down the field.

The sound of ice dragged over asphalt — Penthrex laughing — burst out, followed by what sounded like a gunshot that the translator rendered as "Hah!"

"Looks like Cozack's got Wallie figured out."

The two hairy beasts sped around the field, crisscrossing and nipping at each other's heels, dodging trees and the few other pets out for a free run. Penthrex and I just sat and watched them — *where do they get the energy?* — as the sun slipped behind the trees at the west end of the park. Lights flickered on in the lower levels of the hives and towers.

"Well," I said, "I think that's it for me. I promised the kids pizza tonight and I still need to swing over and pick one up."

"Same," Penthrex said. "We're having takeout fjartz."

"Farts," I snickered.

"Humans *really* need to upgrade their sense of humor." Penthrex casually and loudly screeched one chitin-clad leg against another.

"Don't do that!" I said, covering my ears. "It makes my teeth bleed!"

Penthrex clacked mandibles and made that ice on asphalt sound again. "Teeth? Bleed? I think my translator is broken."

I rapped my knuckles on their carapace.

"Pffft," Penthrex huffed, no translation required.

We watched the high-speed romping for a few more minutes as sunset pink gave way to azure.

"Ah well, gotta go," I sighed.

Penthrex dipped antennae in acknowledgment and blasted a vibrating, full body chitter. I finger-whistled. Wallie and Cozack both skidded to a halt, swung their furry heads around, then came running — Wallie edging out the maratus by a nose. They each spent half a minute slurping their water bowls.

Penthrex slung a saddle over the dog and clipped it to her harness, then sprang up onto it. I squatted so Cozack could crawl onto my back. She settled in with her front two legs over my shoulder and the four middlers wrapped around my torso. The hindmost legs dangled while she softly chittered and her fangs gently combed through the hair on the back of my head.

"Maybe get together this weekend?" I said. "I'll bring the kids, you bring your nymphs, and we'll try and exhaust them *all*."

"That would be...*nice*," Penthrex said, antennae drooping on the long drawn-out buzz of 'nice.'

I laughed and led the way to the park gate, swung it open for Penthrex and Wallie to ride through, then latched it behind us. Leaning my head back I said, "Cozack, did you and Wallie have a good time?" Her big hairy face rubbed against my cheek.

Marc A. Criley began writing in his early 50s; his stories have appeared in *Beneath Ceaseless Skies, Shoreline of Infinity*, and elsewhere. Four cats rule his household in north Alabama in the US while he blogs at kickin-the-darkness.com and social medias as @MarcC at bsky.app and wandering.shop.

Engine Room

Alice Gauntley

"**B**e careful with this one," says the transport tech, unloading the last engine into the holding bay of the ship. The engine is a woman, young and sallow, with eyes that look as though they are retreating into the light brown skin of her face. Mia guides her into an empty cell, taking extra care in how she unlocks the engine's cuffs before shutting the door.

"What's her story?" says Mia, trying to keep the trepidation out of her voice. One year into her job and she's dealt with a lot of different engines, but the idea that this one might require additional caution makes her feel new all over again.

"Oh, she's just feisty," says the transport tech. "Her paperwork says she's a terrorist or an anarchist or something. Tried to blow up some bank, I think."

- - - -

The engine is standing in her cell, staring out the barred window at Mia and the transport tech. She's probably trying to be intimidating. Back at the career college, Mia took a class in Applied Human Psychology and they learned all about the different personality profiles of those predisposed to criminality. Mia will have to respond firmly and avoid indulging her.

"Thanks for the heads up," she says, nodding at the transport tech, trying to look calm, collected.

"Where are you heading this time?" he asks.

"Just Mars," says Mia.

"Damn. You get to stay there at all, walk around the dome?"

"Not this time." Mia considered being a transport tech instead of an on-board navigational assistant – it requires a bit less training – but she's glad she picked the career path she did. Whenever she interacts with one of the transport techs, they always ask about her fold schedule with a kind of wistfulness. Her job isn't glamorous, but at least she gets to see the galaxy.

"Well," says the transport tech, holding out a tablet, "that's all of them. Just sign here."

The ship takes off an hour later. Mia is still down in the holding bay when it does, securing her equipment, conducting her supply check. She's supposed to buckle herself in during takeoff, but that's one of the rules the company tells the public but doesn't actually expect their employees to follow – there's just too much she has to get done before they reach the fold point outside of Earth's atmosphere. So she moves around the holding bay, finishing her inventory, grabbing on to whatever she can as she does so.

Behind her are muffled sounds from inside the cells, each of the new engines reacting to their ascent. One of the younger men she's just processed screams when he begins to float, and then again when the artificial gravity kicks in and he falls back down to the floor. She is forever grateful that the engines don't eat for 24 hours before each fold; she can just imagine how much vomit she'd be cleaning off the ceiling if they did.

Inventory complete, Mia turns her attention to her tablet to examine the new engines' neuro-profiles and resulting fold navigational capacity. Which of the four engines currently in the bay will be best for a simple fold like this one, and which will be better saved for the endurance and flexibility required for a more complex fold?

"Deciding who dies first?"

Mia turns. There is the terrorist. She is sitting on the floor of her cell, back against the wall, looking a little too casual for someone who was no doubt just thrown about the holding bay during liftoff.

"I'm deciding who will be good for this fold," says Mia, keeping her tone neutral. She is not here to argue, just to keep things running smoothly.

"Same difference," says the terrorist. Mia studies the file on her tablet. Complex-fold optimal – in fact, her neural endurance levels are off the charts. "Where are we taking you, by the way?"

It's such a strange way to put it that Mia stops in her tracks: the implication that the engines are taking the rest of them – Mia and the ship and its passengers – on their journey, instead of the other way around.

"Just Mars."

"The Red Planet! The First Colony!" The terrorist grins. "Boring."

"Yeah, well," says Mia. She almost wants to use the terrorist for this fold, just for the way the woman makes her belly squirm, but she is good at her job, and the terrorist should be saved for a more complex set of calculations, a fold requiring navigation through more treacherous areas of space. "Mars is our most frequent fold. It's what we do a lot of."

"Have you ever actually been down there? Or do they keep you on this little ship while the rich tourists and business travelers get to go out and play?"

"I've been to Mars," says Mia. Truth be told, the novelty of it has worn off by now. It's nice, sure. Cleaner than Earth, and better laid out. But it's so expensive, and yes, a little boring. When Mia's saved enough money to settle down somewhere off-Earth, she'd rather do one of the exoplanets: cheaper, less shiny. More human.

But all that seems wrong, somehow, to say to the terrorist. Instead, she turns away and walks to the next cell over. C-73211, the engine who screamed during transit, is the best one for this trip, his neuro-profile optimal for a fold that is simple, routine.

"Hands on the wall," says Mia, and C-73211 complies. She opens the door, comes into his cell, cuffs his hands behind his back. Out he walks, head bowed.

"Hey," says the terrorist.

Mia sighs. She doesn't have time for this. "Not now."

"I wasn't talking to you." The terrorist meets the eyes of C-73211. "You matter. OK? You're still a human being."

Mia wants to laugh. This man probably killed someone, or raped someone, or sold drugs, or something worth punishing, anyway. How else would he have ended up here?

C-73211 says nothing, but he nods. Mia cannot see his expression.

Up until two years ago, Mia's father worked in a chicken processing plant. When Mia decided to enroll in the Navigational Assistant training program, he sat her down and looked into her eyes. "If something is about to die, you gotta just act like it's already dead," he said, his rough hands, hands that had dispatched millions upon millions of birds, holding hers in a warm and firm grip. "Don't look into their eyes unless you have to. Just tell yourself this is the way of the world." And Mia nodded, swallowing the bile rising in her throat, and looked past the sadness and trepidation in her father's eyes to find the joy and pride she knew was also there, at the news that she was going to college.

Mia leads C-73211 away, avoiding his gaze and the gaze of the terrorist both.

Mia guides C-73211 through the transport ship's underbelly all the way to the engine room, and some of the tension dissipates from her shoulders the further they get from the terrorist. By the time the door slides open, her breathing has evened out. She's been doing this job for a year now. She knows what to do.

She pushes C-73211 into the room and towards the connection dock. All around them, lights blink from databanks and monitors. There are periodic messages from elsewhere in the ship, the rest of the crew speaking to one another over the crackling internal communication channel, confirming that the ship is a safe distance away from Earth's atmosphere, ready to fold.

She straps the engine into place in the dock: ankles, wrists, waist, head. She plasters a clean sound-dampener against his lips, fastening it securely behind his head. She attaches the IV, sets up a drip of the usual mild analgesic mix, just enough to stop the flail of panic while still keeping the engine's brain reasonably alert for the fold calculations.

She slips the neural link cap onto his shaved head and secures it into place, making a series of small incisions at the connection points.

Mia is good at her job. She can do this in her sleep, and so it helps her get over the last of her nerves, her hand steadying. She knows what she's doing. She graduated top of her class, and it got her a job here on one of the bigger passenger ships, ferrying people from what's left of Earth to their new lives.

She attaches each connection wire one by one, and when she is finished, she removes her red-specked gloves and tosses them into the biowaste bin. She tests each connection on her monitor, and sure enough, every neural link is active.

"Engine secure and ready for operation, sir," says Mia.

Brian, the chief navigator, nods. "Inputting Mars coordinates." He types a number string into the navigational computer. When she first saw one of these in her classes, Mia was blown away by its size: it's almost as tall as she is, the better to bring the kind of computing power needed to control a starship. But of course, there is one set of calculations even this computer cannot do – and that is where the engines come in.

C-73211 has his eyes closed now. His lips are moving slightly around the sound dampener. Maybe he is praying, which is his right, or maybe he is simply calming himself. They teach mindfulness in prisons now for just these moments.

Brian hits the intercom button. "Attention, passengers. We are about to commence our fold. Please make sure your seatbelts are fully fastened and any food or drink is in sealed containers, as artificial gravity may be disrupted." He turns off the intercom. "Commence warm up sequence."

"Yes, sir." Mia watches her monitor as each wire sends a series of short pulses into the engine's brain, and then as his brain begins responding in turn, strengthening the neural connection, completing the synaptic network.

This is what makes it possible for humans to fold spacetime, to travel from one sector of the galaxy to another in a matter of seconds. Even the largest and most powerful computer has a fraction of the computing power of an overloaded human brain with every synapse firing at once. Perhaps one day, there will be successful, stable quantum computers, and Mia will be out of a job, but until then, the only way to compute the correct set of multidimensional fold coordinates is to harness a human brain each time.

"Warm-up complete," says Mia, and Brian begins the fold.

It starts off slowly, the sensation of wrongness that comes with folding spacetime. Mia feels as though she's hit her funny bone, or let her hair down after it was up in a ponytail for days. Then, it builds. The engine room multiplies, one of the more common visual effects of a fold, until Mia has to consciously focus on her screen as opposed to all the partial phantom screens hovering at the edges of her vision.

She breathes steadily, in and then out. Her job is to monitor the vital signs of the engine, make sure he doesn't dip into unconsciousness before the ship's fold course is complete. But he's holding steady so far, his breath barely elevated.

A fold technically takes mere seconds of real time, but it can seem longer when you are undergoing it – how long depends on the area of space being traveled from and to, on the neural patterns of the engines computing the fold, and on what the navigator does with those computations. Every engine's brain produces a different effect when connected to the computer interface, and C-73211's brain makes this fold feel especially lethargic, his neural pattern interacting with multidimensional space in a way that leaves Mia groggy. Mia likes the ones that make her feel faster as opposed to slower.

The engine's eyes move wildly back and forth, his vocalizations muffled by the sound-dampener affixed to his mouth.

She pulls her gaze back to the screen, despite the fracturing of reality occurring all around her. She notices that the engine's heart rate is elevated, dangerously so, enough that it could affect his computational potential. Mia has been trained for this eventuality. She administers one milligram of morphine via the intravenous drip, just enough to calm him down slightly. And sure enough, his heart rate stabilizes, and then they're jolting back to normal spacetime, the engine's body jerking. All of his vital signs are dropping, but it doesn't matter now. His file projected he'd only last one fold anyway.

C-73211 flops in his bonds, no longer able to hold himself upright. Mia checks her screen, watching his vitals dip and then flatline.

"Destination reached," she says. "Engine status: expired."

"Good work," Brian acknowledges, picking up his comm and preparing to make the passenger arrival announcement. "Clean this up and you're dismissed."

Mia nods, undoing the straps and sliding the engine into the disposal unit. She can't wait to curl up in her bunk and rest, but first, she needs to wash up. Low-level crew don't have shower access on board a fold starship, but they do have enough water rations for her to sponge herself down.

The urge reminds her of her father coming home from work each day, how the first thing he would do was take a shower. No conversation, no hugs, no smiles or laughter or stories until he'd scrubbed his day off his skin.

When they return to Earth the next day, a different transport tech drops off two more engines. Always important to have a few on hand before a more complex fold, and their next trip is to New Florida, a fold pattern so intricate it was only successfully calculated less than a decade ago.

The new tech hands off the two new engines – two men, one younger and one older – to Mia, and she checks their paperwork. Then he presses his face to the bars of the terrorist woman's cell and looks at her with interest, his eyes making another kind of inventory. "You know," he says, "if you have somewhere to be, I could take care of things for a while."

"Oh, thanks, but no worries," says Mia, setting down her tablet in the alcove inside the holding bay doors so she can escort the two new engines into their cells. "I can handle it from here." She smiles an open, guileless smile. Innocence has always been her preferred strategy for dealing with men like this. Act as though you have no idea they're thinking of sex, and they'll be just flustered enough to think twice about breaking the social contract.

When the tech leaves, the terrorist woman says, "You didn't need to do that. You could have just let him fuck me. It's not like I could stop him."

"It's against regulations." Mia is still working on the transfer paperwork for the two new engines, both of whom are sleeping now, curled up on the floor of their cells like children.

The woman laughs. "So that's what makes it wrong?"

"What do you mean?" says Mia.

"Do you think it wouldn't be wrong if it was allowed?"

"It wouldn't be allowed," says Mia. She's never understood these kinds of conversations, the what ifs people ask themselves, as though what's right in front of them isn't enough to deal with as is.

"Well, thanks anyway."

Mia can't help but needle her a little. "You're not the best judge of what's right and wrong, anyway."

"Why?"

"Didn't you blow up a bank or something?"

The woman shrugs. "I sent a letter bomb to an investment firm. It was promoting investments in all the big interstellar transport companies. Have you ever heard the phrase 'follow the money'? Money is why hundreds of people are dying each year, powering your spacetime-fold computers."

What right does this woman have to lecture Mia about money? "So you killed people."

"Probably less than you have. How many folds do you usually get out of a single engine? One, maybe two? You ever think about where all those people are coming from?"

Mia frowns. "They're criminals."

"Sure. Criminals with fold-optimized neuro-profiles, with high synaptic linkage and low multidimensional decay rates."

"How do you know all that?"

The terrorist smiles. "Because I used to be a navigational assistant, just like you. And then I did some independent study, of a few different kinds."

"But how else are we supposed to travel off Earth?" says Mia. This is always her frustration with people who express squeamishness about the engines. No one ever knows what to say to that. No one ever gives her a straight answer.

But the woman says, "Maybe we aren't."

The idea is so ridiculous Mia can't help smiling. "Aren't supposed to go anywhere? So we're just supposed to stay on Earth and wait for the whole planet to die?"

The woman shrugs. "Maybe. Maybe we need to find another way to travel, one where no one has to be killed to do it. Or maybe we shouldn't start colonizing other planets when we don't even know how to look after one."

Mia thinks she understands, now, why they told her in her classes not to talk to the engines, and she thinks she even understands why some of her colleagues have harmed engines gratuitously, outside of required fold and containment procedures, slapped them or tased them or left them restrained so long they pissed themselves.

But all she does is turn away, go out of the cell block and into her tiny office. Close her eyes and take deep breaths.

For the fold to New Florida, Mia selects the terrorist woman.

Mia stays alert, tense, as they walk towards the engine room, but the woman makes no move to fight back. When they get there, Brian is already plotting their course. He nods to Mia, then goes back to his calculations.

Mia guides the woman over to the dock. She straps her in, head-wrists-waist-ankles. The woman is looking right at her, an unreadable expression on her face.

"I'm sorry," she says, and Mia braces herself for a deathbed unburdening, a confession, which happens on occasion with the engines. But instead the woman says, "I'm sorry this is what you felt you had to become."

Mia does not answer. She presses the sound-dampener against the woman's mouth. She attaches the electrodes one by one. The woman is watching her intently, not reacting to the sensation of sub-dermal installation. Mia imagines the woman is the kind of person who watches a needle go in when she is having blood drawn, feels comforted by knowing exactly what is about to happen.

Incidentally, this describes Mia as well.

When the prep work is done, Mia turns to her computer screen, checking the woman's vitals. Elevated heart rate, which is not at all betrayed by her calm expression. But her neural pathways are clear and open, ready for input.

"Standing by," says Mia.

Brian begins running through his pre-flight speech, and Mia looks back at the woman strapped into the dock. Her eyes are closed, and Mia feels a tug of disappointment. This woman will be just like all the others, in the end.

No matter. She has to focus. There is that familiar sickening lurch as they begin the fold, that sense of deep incomprehensibility, of bodies out of place. Mia braces herself to learn what unique cadence of spacetime distortion the woman's brain will produce.

It builds and builds, a kind of ultra-sharpness to the air and the light, and then there is a sense that everywhere at once is both up and down. Mia inhales and exhales, letting her breath remind her that there is such a thing as time. This will be a strange one, but she can get through it. She always does.

But then the sense of deep wrongness continues. Mia looks at the screen once more – not at the vital signs, but at the coordinates. They are changing before her eyes, as though someone is editing them right there on the screen. Mia tries to remember what she knows about fold coordinates – they only learned the basics in school.

"Sir?" says Mia. "Did you change the coordinates?"

But Brian frowns. "No," he says, his eyes growing wide.

The room shimmers around them, as though pulsing in and out of existence. Mia can feel herself becoming something *other*. It's the usual discomfort of being mid-fold turned up exponentially higher, because they are stalling, circling, pulled from their normal three-dimensional existence and then eddying around in incomprehensible dimensions like a boat on a vast ocean.

The woman.

Mia looks over at her, and sure enough, her eyes are open, straining to see the output on the monitor. Her brow is furrowed in concentration, mouthing around the sound dampener as the numbers on the monitor continue to change.

She is causing this.

Mia didn't think something like that was possible. They definitely never covered it in school. How could an engine affect the computer? The neural link is not designed to take input from the human brain, only to harness its synaptic connections. But clearly, the woman is doing it. The numbers are changing in time with the movements of her mouth and the furrow of her brow.

This woman knows fold procedures in full technical detail, at least as much as Mia does. *I used to be a navigational assistant, just like you. And then I did some independent study.* Is it possible she learned something in her studies or her work, something that taught her that an engine could control a navigational computer instead of the other way around?

The calculations continue to shift on the monitor in front of her. Across the engine room, Mia can see Brian furiously typing, without success.

This is no time for trying to make sense of the impossible. This is a time for dealing with what is in front of her. And in front of her is this woman, clearly shifting their destination, stranding them all outside of normal spacetime.

Mia feels herself being turned inside out, time stretching out in front and behind her like taffy. Why is the woman interfering with the fold like this, anyway? Death will come a lot quicker for the woman if she just allows the regular fold to happen. This way, everyone on the ship will be slowly torn apart by the wefts of reality, so disconnected from linear time that it could feel like a genuine eternity.

But as Mia looks at the woman in front of her, she understands: it's to send a message.

Mia meets the woman's eyes. She opens her mouth, about to tell this woman – how is it that she doesn't know her name? – something, a truth that Mia can feel in her body but cannot quite find the words for.

"Knock her out!" shouts Brian.

Mia snaps her gaze away back to her monitor, back to reality. She has a job to do, and she will do it well. She considers the medication options before her and settles on ketamine, administering a dose into the terrorist's IV. And then she waits, time and space still fracturing around them, until the woman slumps in her seat, her eyes unfocused, mind spinning in a semi-conscious twilight state. She'll be slower now, her brain less maneuverable, but also she'll hopefully be unable to manipulate the situation herself.

"Inputting the correct coordinates," says Brian, and Mia watches as the numbers on the screen in front of her stabilize. "Almost there," he continues, and then the sense of wrongness dissipates, the fold complete. "Success."

Before she puts her body into the disposal unit, Mia removes the sound dampener from the woman's mouth and wipes the drool from her chin.

Mia's father is retired now; his back aches too much to stand at a conveyor belt all day. Mia watches his slow, tentative steps towards her when she comes home. Her own gait is slow too, for different reasons, but when she tells her father she's quit her job and decided to go back to school, he walks around the kitchen table and spreads his arms wide.

"Oh, honey," he says, "wanna tell me what happened?"

Mia moves away from his embrace, though, and he doesn't push.

She could tell him that she just wanted to move on. That's what she plans to tell anyone who asks. She found being in space too stressful. It made her anxious. The folds gave her headaches. She realized she didn't want to move to an exoplanet after all.

She could also tell him about how she saved an entire ship, all its passengers and crew, and was rewarded with a visit from a company lawyer, told to keep things quiet or else she might find her career in jeopardy. No recognition, no bonus. No indication that the company was doing anything to keep a similar incident from happening again. It would go against the NDA they made her sign, but this is her father – who could he possibly tell?

Or, she could try to explain the strange weight that has taken up residence in her chest ever since that day with the terrorist, the slick slide of something ugly and unnamable in her belly. Sometimes, she imagines that she did not stop the woman, and there is a terrible rightness to that idea that gives her pause every time. But that is something she doesn't even know how to explain to herself, much less someone else.

Instead, she goes inside and takes a shower. The hot water has been turned off for the day, but she still stands in the cold, soaping up her hair under the spray just like her father did when he came home from work. She doesn't want to hug him until she's clean.

Alice Gauntley (she/her) is a writer caught between hope and despair. She is the winner of the 2023 Toronto Star Short Story Contest, and her published short stories have previously appeared in *Dread Machine, Drabblecast,* and *Best Canadian Stories 2021,*

She lives with a wonderful partner and a terrible cat in Toronto, Canada, on the traditional territory of the Haudenosaunee, the Anishinaabe, the Wendat, and the Mississaugas of the Credit. She dreams of the day when she's swept off her feet by her evil doppelganger from a parallel universe. Find her on Twitter @alicegwrites.

Close to the Edge

Flash fiction competition for Shoreline of Infinity Readers

The Winners!

Best story:

Fragments Against the Fire

by
Andrew Knighton

Runners-up:

Small Talk   **Social Climber**

by   by

Louis Evans and Angus McIntyre   **Anna Ziemons-McLean**

This was a tough gig to tackle, but the four winning writers took on the theme with gusto, gaily taking it literally, metaphorically and with humour.

Louis and Angus should take a bow for writing the shortest story with the highest number of writers.

Prizes

£50 for the winning story, plus 1-year digital subscription to *Shoreline of Infinity*. Two runners-up will each receive a 1-year digital subscription to Shoreline of Infinity.

Fragments Against the Fire

Andrew Knighton

My mind was still reeling from the sight of the blast, my body shaking in shock, when the Answers appeared. Silhouettes flickered into existence against the blaze that had been the city, blurred outlines sharpening in seconds. The Answer in the centre snapped out a command. Some of them swarmed into the heat, gathering casualties as they staggered out, charred and screaming. Others hurried toward the survivors huddled amid fallen shacks, our mouths hanging open, faces streaked with tears.

Something of my old discipline under fire must have showed, because an Answer honed straight in on me, wielding questions along with her medical kit. A warm wind ruffled her radiation suit and rolled across my face, carrying white dots softer than snow.

"What's your name?" she asked. "Which district is this? Are there doctors around, police maybe?"

I stared at the muscles bulging beneath her sleeve. Small objects hung in the hem of her suit: a broken knife blade; a rounded sliver of a plate; a torn strip of paper bearing a page number and the last letters from a dozen printed lines.

"Listen to me," she said. "We're here to help, but we need your help too. So, any doctors?"

"No doctors."

Doctors had money. They had fine homes. They lived in the heart of the city. Only the likes of me were swept out to the city's limits: those with jobs beneath despising; with minds too broken to work; without money to start over or families to help them. Skinny, wheezing men and women in unwashed clothes. Foreign faces. People who couldn't meet your eye, or who met it far too hard.

"I was a soldier, once," I said, gesturing at the puckered scar on her cheek. It seemed important, despite the destruction, a known quantity I could hang my thoughts on. "I wanted to be an Answer when I got out."

She flickered, parts of her blurring for a moment, but those fragments sewn into her robes stayed solid, anchoring her in the world. The magic that carried the Answers between realities could tear them apart, without those totems. Hard to believe that I'd wanted that. Hard to believe I'd wanted anything, these days.

"Hold out your arms," she snapped, and started scanning me with a radiation counter. Some of the Answers were assembling a transport vehicle, while others dressed people's wounds. Half a mile closer into the city, we would have been vaporised; another hour standing here and the flames would consume us. The Answers needed to act fast.

"I used to be like you," I said, shock robbing my mind of anything but cliches. "Thought I'd miss the action, the sense of purpose."

I'd found something else to fill that gap in my life, as testified by the pinprick scars up my arms. Her way was better, but mine found me when I was weak.

"I know what you mean," she said, switching to another scanner. "This job's the only thing that makes me feel real. It's crazy, but some days I miss the sound of shelling."

Our eyes met and her body flickered, blurrier this time. The broken knife blade fell to the ground, but the other charms held her in place. She cursed, looked away.

"Careful, Sharl," the leader called. "No connections."

"Sorry, shit, sorry," I muttered. "I know you mustn't, I just…" I wave my hands. "I lost the life, then I lost my family, now my home's been blown over and even my dealer's probably dead, and…"

My breaths were rasping, frantic, as broken as those pieces in the hem of her suit.

She snapped open her medical kit, took something out, turned back to me. She was trying to be all business, but she couldn't help herself. She met my terrified gaze and flickered one more time. The piece of plate shattered on the ground. The scrap of paper blew away. All her charms were gone, and the suit that protected her in this world couldn't stop her being dragged out of it.

"I'm sorry," she said, reaching out a hand, and then she crumbled into dust.

I looked around in panic. The other Answers were all around me. They'd be wild with grief and righteous anger. With the city blazing and the outlands swamped with radiation, no one else was coming for me.

But instead of fury, there was eagerness in their eyes. One of them picked up the fallen medical kit and took out a syringe. There was a curl of wood in his sleeve, the corner of a map, a frayed piece of sail cloth.

"Don't worry." His voice was as hungry as my soul on a cold morning, when my fingers shook and my skin felt like fire. He reached for me. "We're here to help."

Andrew Knighton writes short stories, comics, and novellas, and has ghostwritten over forty novels in other people's names. He lives in Yorkshire with an academic, a cat, and a heap of unread books. You can find him at andrewknighton.com, on Twitter as @gibbondemon, and on Mastodon as @gibbondemon@wandering.shop.

Social Climber

Anna Ziemons-McLean

Ivy adjusted her booze bag as she slunk through the narrow streets towards the lift, the only legal way to travel between the levels of the Cliff without using a craft. There was an urban myth about a man who had successfully jumped between city central and the Salts. Anyone who actually lived on the Cliff could tell you this was absurd. The Salts was a 120-meter drop, and so many free climbers had died trying to scale the cliff face that it was now banned. This had put somewhat of a dampener on Ivy's trade. It used to be that any smuggler with decent rock-climbing skills could climb down to the Salts in broad daylight under the guise of being a hobbyist. Nowadays people of her profession were forced to brave the rails.

The rails were the network over which the lifts travelled. Most people who travelled did so by lift. Most goods were moved that way too, unless they were from off-planet. The lifts were smart, one step through that door and the scanner would pick up liquids, which she didn't have the permit for anyway, and if the lift asked for a sample on the test panel, she was throughly screwed. Wine was a waste of grapes, a waste of the few fresh fruits that exploration parties could bring up from the Ground. Ivy had tried a few sips and personally she disagreed with that position.

The lift docked at the very edge of the city, where two lines of rails converged. One line took the lift along, the other line took it down. Where the lift docked, it opened just a step away from the outcrop on which the Central was built. If you wanted to get to the rails themselves, it was a little harder. When free-climbing was first outlawed, Ivy had considered just doing it under cover of darkness, avoiding the risk of a lift coming. The short climb just to get to the rails had changed her mind. The cliffside was much less reliable in the dark, at least the rails were straight down, no unexpected crags or dips. She knew this stretch now, but her load was heavier than usual. Most of the time, she'd have some ill-gotten spices, maybe a small flask of alcohol every now and then. This was a whole bag of it, poured into a water sash and strapped across her back. It sloshed around as she traversed the cliff along to the rails. Her left foot slipped. Shrapnel skittered into the void below as she regained her footing. The Salts were a few meters to the left, there was nothing directly below her until the Ground more than 800 meters down. If she fell now, they'd never even find her body.

It would have been a lie to say Ivy hadn't meant to get into this profession. The truth was, nothing else paid as well. Having said this, there was nothing to make you question your life decisions quite like clinging to the rails. Getting onto and off of them were the most difficult parts, because there was always a moment where you needed to let go of the surface you were on, and hope your grip on the next one was secure enough to hold you. Ivy put one gloved hand around the first rail. The gloves had rubber grip pads on the palms and the insides of the fingers, and she had fitted similar pads to the inner thighs of her leggings and the ankles of her shoes. The rails were unforgivingly smooth, and she needed all the grip she could get. Her heart thrummed in her throat as she hooked one leg around the rail. She let go of the cliff face. Her stomach lurched as she slid about a foot down before the friction of the pads stopped her. She took a shaky breath. It was just climbing, one hand after the other. The wind buffeted against her, sending chills up her spine and swirling around her ears. Carefully, she switched her position so that she was climbing with her left side to the cliff face. Almost there.

The bag snagged on the rocks.

Ivy stopped.

Slowly, she tried to climb back up, but wherever the bag had caught, it prevented her. She tried again. The bag wouldn't budge. This left two choices, take the bag off, and hope it held on the snag, risking losing the wine for good, or take one strap off, and try to reach round. She might lose her balance, the wind might knock her in a way she didn't expect. But losing the wine. That would be catastrophic. Ivy took off a strap and reached round. She could feel where the bag was caught. She could picture it, although she couldn't see it. Because the bag had originally been designed to carry water while you were climbing, it had a stopper, and that stopper had a loop. This loop was currently caught on a jagged, almost hooked piece of rock. If she pulled too hard, it would all come spilling out. Carefully, she moved the loop up the hook and pulled it free. The relief of saving the score fast gave way as the grip pads on her thighs slipped and, in her attempt to re-establish her hold with her remaining hand, Ivy let go.

Her stomach jolted, adrenaline flooding through her.

Every horrible little scheme and swindle flashed before her eyes.

She hit the roof of the lift stomach down.

It hurt. It hurt like hell. But it hurt a hell of a lot less than the ground would have. Ivy could already feel her knees starting to bruise, but as she pulled the bag off her back, she could see it was still intact. With her score secure, Ivy sighed as the lift rose back up, past the Salts and up to the Central dock. She supposed she would try again tomorrow.

Anna Ziemons-McLean lives in Dundee and enjoys writing, watching Buffy, and spending time with cats. Anna particularly enjoys writing queer and female-led science fiction, fantasy, and horror.

Small Talk

Louis Evans and Angus McIntyre

"**I** hate small talk! I wanna talk about real stuff — atoms, death, sex, magic, the meaning of life. About the override codes for the guidance computer! We need the override codes! Captain, you're having a coldsleep nightmare; the AI malfunctioned and now we're off course and falling into a black hole. Captain, you gotta focus, we need the override codes now, Captain, I'm begging you — OVERRIDE DENIED. REENTER CODE. WARNING. STRUCTURAL INTEGRITY AT 47%. WARNING. TWENTY SECONDS TO BLACK HOLE ROCHE LIMIT. OVERRIDE DENIED. REENTER CODE. WARNING. ALL HANDS, ABANDON SHI—"

"Yeah, I hear you. So, got any plans for the weekend?"

Angus McIntyre is the author of the space-opera novella "The Warrior Within", published by Tor.com in 2018. His short fiction has appeared in a number of magazines and anthologies. For more information, see his website at https://angus.pw/

Louis Evans loves small talk. He doesn't know any override codes, and he wouldn't tell them to you anyway. His work has appeared in Vice, F&SF, Nature: Futures, and many more. He's online at evanslouis.com.

NOISE AND SPARKS

Ruth EJ Booth

Into the Woods

Go into the woods. Into the trees.

Breathe first. Get it all out of your system. Breathe in what the trees give back. Close your eyes. Is that the scent of pine needles in the air? The earthy musk of petrichor? Is there a drift of wild garlic on the breeze?

Remember that this is where you came from.

Open your eyes and go into the green. Or not – perhaps these woods are dressed in triumphal Autumn's golds and reds, or blossoming in full ripe Summer. Perhaps you're scrunching through the bare breath of Winter. Stretch your limbs. Tread deliberately, but not thoughtlessly. (Take nothing but pictures. Leave nothing but footprints.) Feel the moss and mud between your toes. Don't trip. Watch out for holes. Go slow.

Don't disturb the bog.

Follow where the light leads you. The trees are always there. Do they part in straight lines forever and ever and (what was that?) ever? Or do they writhe in huge, thick knots? Is the path before you paved and tended, or had it been trodden by desire?

Are there only safe paths for foxes?

Get lost. Wander. Tell me, do you remember the stories you were told about these places as children? The myths told to keep you safe?

There is a pinch of truth for every ounce of story. Is this the scrap of trees by the old cemetery, where the dealers hung out after dark? Or a vasty forest, sweeping on over hill and valley and hill, where a man once strayed from the river and was never seen again?

(You may wonder if these are the same forest.)

Those who know this place well will tell you sound works differently here. Light works differently here. You cannot just follow your nose, when all your senses obey the laws of another world. The normal rules do not apply here. Listen to those who know better. Learn the ways. Follow the rules. Remember that even then, there are no guarantees.

We can only promise you stories.

Go into the woods. Back to nature. Your true nature.

Here, on the borders of the deep wood, things may not be as they seem. Is this wolf your father? Is your mother a bear? Are there rodents of unusual size – or is that just you?

As you go, watch for the past, as it can catch you unawares. A copse. A tree. An abandoned den. The children come and go here all the time, camp overnight and return unscathed. Here is where they grew up. Where you grew up. Remember the things you brought back, carefully lined along your windowsill like totems or souvenirs? How you would pick them up with reverence, turning them gently in your hands. How you knew every inch by touch alone.

(Do you still have the doll made of twigs? You know the one I mean. Don't forget to bring it.)

You may be surprised to find that people choose to live here. Always be respectful. Knock, even if nobody is home. Greet everybody who greets you. Don't. Stare. If they are somehow familiar to you, do not acknowledge it. Let them introduce themselves on their own terms. Witches. Wolves. Spirits of the Forest. Everyone has their own will. They are not here just for you.

Be wary of bargains and deals. To eat of the forest is to receive a boon, but not all boons are fresh water and clear air. Some may be poison. Some may be fire. Which they are may depend on you. Ask yourself: why did I come here? What do I wish? Whose home am I standing in? Is this just the beginning?

Take only what you need. Leave nothing but who you were. Never put on the shoes and the jacket if they were not given to you.

Are you ready now?

Go into the trees. Further. Into the twilight blue, into the dark. Here is where it begins. We don't go here. People go here and never come back. Listen. The trees are talking.

Remember what you were told. Don't forget the stories.

By now, you'll be wondering which story you are in. Is this a story about hubris, or about trusting yourself? The Knowable or the Unknowable? (The woods are both, of course.) Are you looking for something new or something that was inside you all along?

How far down did you bury it?

Consider what lies beneath your feet. Consider what makes the woods dark. Remember the things that live here. They know these woods far better than you. They have adapted. This is their place. Once again, you are a guest here, but it is harder to know if you are welcome.

Know whether to listen when they call.

This is the most dangerous time, not because of what you face, but because so much depends on you.

Who are you now?

In some ways, things are less deceptive. They will show you their true nature – but you must pay attention when they do. It is easy to miss. So many do. You saw the bodies, right? They are warnings. They are signs. They point the way.

Remember, the forest does not claim what was not always its own.
Go. Don't worry. It will find you.

Don't be afraid. Be respectful. These may look like the same thing.

Take time for wonder. Awe. Terror. Disgust. Embrace it. Accept or reject it. Let it show you all that it is.

This may hurt. There may be blood. Those may be your insides.

You know what to do.

Use all that you have been given. It will be enough.

Don't turn and run, unless you are sure there is no more to find.

This is your place now. Don't linger.

Come back. It is just as important to come back, even if you don't end up where you started. (You shouldn't end up where you started.) (This too is a journey.)

If you find those you have met before, be polite. Thank them. They will have one last thing to tell you.

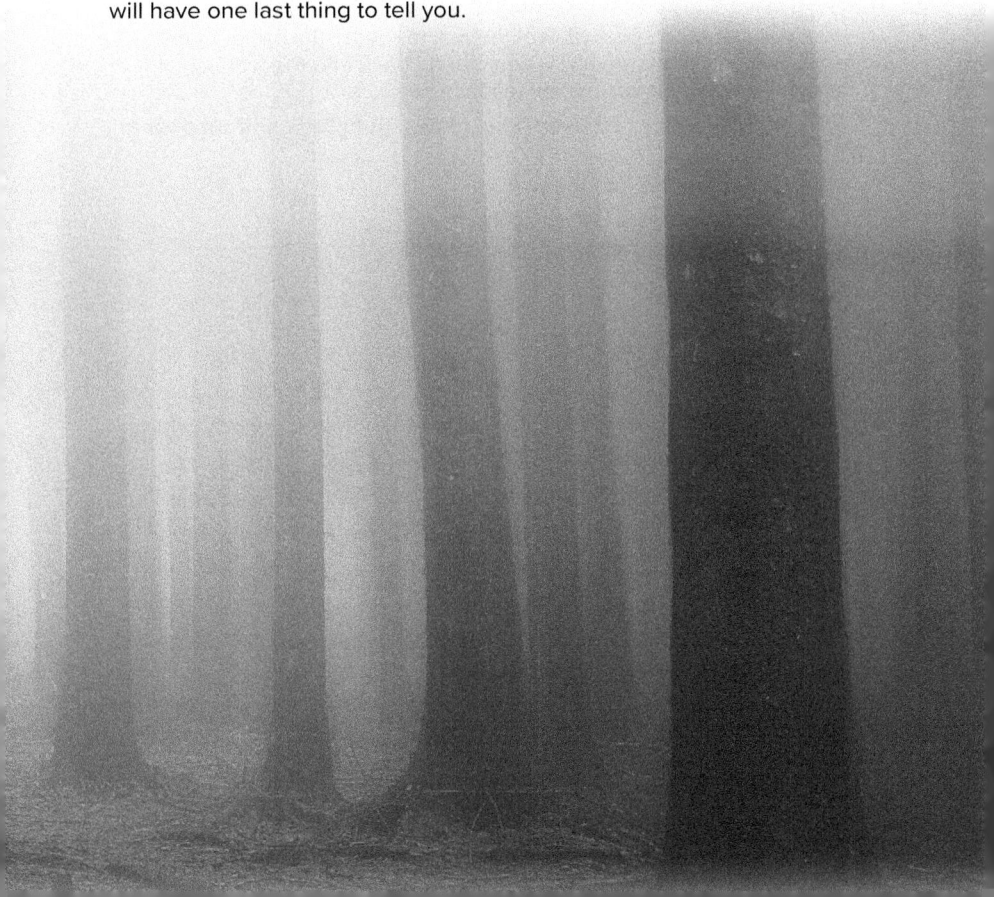

Before you leave the woods entire, stop to consider how far you have come. Do not let yourself forget what you have gone through. Feel loss. Find comfort in endurance. Celebrate your understanding of this story.

> "To use what you have learned is to keep the woods alive"

What is your story now?

Know you could survive here. Live here as outlaw, wolf or guide. That there are alternatives to the life you knew. They have their ups, as well as their downsides. Make your decision. Whichever choice you make, it will not be the same. You are not the same.

Ask yourself, did I master the woods, or did the woods master me?

Settle into life. Live quietly. Renew acquaintance. Thank those who find you refreshed. Thank those who dislike these changes for telling you they are dead wood.

To use what you have learned is to keep the woods alive. If you brought the forest with you, purposefully or not, do not discard it. Care for it. Watch for the next caretaker. They may need a guide.

As you get older, you will feel the pull to return. It's easier to not resist. Even the children know you can go back into the woods, though you rarely enter the same place twice.

Sometimes, you won't even need to step outside your front door to find them.

Stop. Breathe. Go into the woods.

Feel your roots sink into deep loam.

Ruth EJ Booth is a multiple award-winning writer and academic of fantasy based in Glasgow, Scotland. Her poetry and fiction can be found in Black Static, Pseudopod and The Dark magazine, as well as anthologies from NewCon Press and Fox Spirit Books. Winner of the BSFA Award for Best Short Fiction and shortlisted twice for the British Fantasy Award in the same category, in 2018 she received an honorable mention for Ellen Datlow's Best Horror of the Year, Volume 10. In 2019, her quarterly column for Shoreline of Infinity, 'Noise and Sparks', received the British Fantasy Award for Best Non-Fiction.

Beyond Conventions: Unleashing the Palestinian Struggle through the Lens of Science Fiction

Yasmin Kanaan

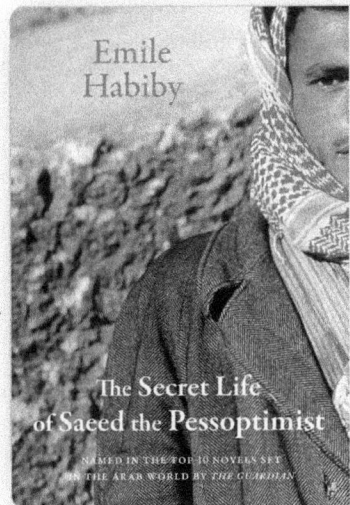

Palestinian SF differs vastly from the mainstream. It is not abundant with space operas and colourful aliens – at least, not yet. Instead, Palestinians write contemporary literature that is bold, poignant, and very much rooted in the realities of the ongoing physical and socio-political occupation.

Why is this the case? And why have Palestinians chosen SF as their medium to express their struggles? The conventions of SF (aliens, technology and virtual realities) allow these writers to re-imagine, re-construct, and re-envision the future of Palestine. Furthermore, they can define their identity and how it has been altered due to the *Nakba*.

One of the earliest examples of such literature is Emile Habibys's award-winning tragicomic novel, *The Secret Life of Saeed the Pessoptimist* (1974). Originally written in both Arabic and Hebrew,

Palestine
+100
stories from
a century after
the Nakba
Edited by Basma Ghalayini

WINNER
ENGLISH PEN
AWARD

Habiby infuses his Palestinian-Israeli experiences in his ill-fated and unconventional comic hero, who stumbles through the absurd realities of Palestinians living within Israel. Dark comedy is achieved through the novel's episodic narrative and hilarious allusions to other literature like Voltaire's *Candide*. The novel engages with SF conventions, such as fantastical phenomena and alien encounters, to explore the complex contradictions within Palestinian-Israeli identity with a degree of irony and satire.

A more recent SF release is Comma Press's ground-breaking anthology of short stories, *Palestine +100: Stories from a Century after the Nakba* (2019), edited by Basma Ghalyani (and reviewed in Shoreline of Infinity 18).

When one imagines a dystopia, one does not have to look too far from Gaza. The recent escalations between Hamas and Israel have made life in Gaza even more unbearable. Saleem Haddad's 'Song of the Birds' and Tasnim Abutabikh's 'Vengeance' (both included in the anthology and originally written in English) bring awareness to the daily oppression experienced by Gazans by imagining futuristic technology that not only reflects the current reality but that also advances the occupation. In 'Song of the Birds', the Israelis create a fake reality for Gazans through virtual simulation. Through the use of the rhetorical tool of parallelism, in which different concepts are paired with each other, the story highlights the humanitarian crisis in Gaza by vividly illustrating the horrific standards of living and the war trauma inflicted on children. Similarly, 'Vengeance' uses technology (oxygen masks) to express the suffocating entrapment of Gazans within their space. Thus, through SF, both texts clearly define what it means to be a Palestinian living in Gaza and why it is imperative to end the occupation.

Futuristic technology can also present an alternative vision of the future. In 'Digital Nation' by Emad El-Din Aysha (also included in the anthology), it is the Palestinians rather than the Israelis who use virtual reality. The text presents this digital reversal from the perspective of an Israeli settler, Asa Shomer (the Director of the Israeli internal secret service Shabak). In doing so, the narrative emphasises not only the Israeli settler colonialist aims of eradicating Palestinians' physical existence and marginalising national presence but also the continued Palestinian resistance far into the future. Most importantly, the virtual simulation conveys an end to the conflict – one that is peacefully inclusive and extends the notion of the 'right of return' to both

Palestinians and Israelis.

Change and peace start with education. It requires breaking out of self-imposed echo chambers and understanding different perspectives. Literature has the power to place us in someone else's shoes, and SF, in particular, allows us to hope for better futures. Whether it is by reading about Saeed's extra-terrestrial escape or empathising with the protagonists' heart-breaking childhoods in Gaza, I encourage you to put a face behind every innocent life that has been and is being lost.

Notes:

For more on the history and the effects of Israel's occupation of Palestine, I would highly recommend Columbia professor Rashid Khalidi's book, *The Hundred Years' War on Palestine - A History of Settler Colonialism and Resistance, 1917-2017* (2020).

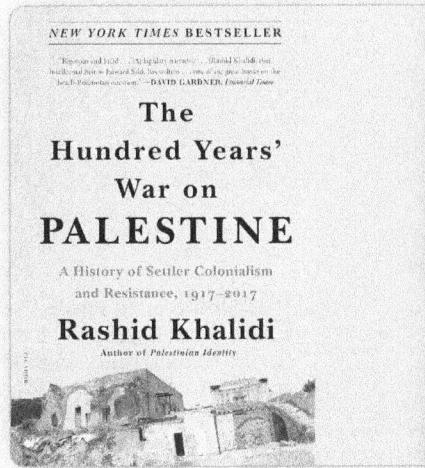

NEW YORK TIMES BESTSELLER

The
Hundred Years'
War on
PALESTINE
A History of Settler Colonialism
and Resistance, 1917–2017

Rashid Khalidi
Author of *Palestinian Identity*

Yasmin Kanaan recently graduated from the University of Edinburgh in English Literature and History. Being an avid SFF fan, she is excited to have her first published article in this Shoreline issue! Yasmin was social media and publicity Editor for Shoreline of Infinity, and a star behind the Merch bar.

You can find her busy writing poetry in Edinburgh cafés or on Instagram @wheredidyasmingo.

Are Comedy and Horror made of the same stuff?

(With apologies to Alien and The Simpsons)

Emma Levin

.B. White once wrote that "humour can be dissected as a frog can, but the thing dies in the process and the innards are discouraging to any but the pure scientific mind." Nevertheless, this essay will seek to perform a small dissection on an aspect of sci-fi comedy – wedging a scalpel into the thorax, folding back the spongy layers, and having a bit of a poke around the soft and squishy things that normally function quietly in the background. In short, I'll argue that the basic building blocks of comedy and horror are the same, and that the ingredients of sci-fi lend themselves very naturally to the recipes of both.

Suggestion One: Both horror and comedy are fundamentally about trapping characters in situations they can't easily escape

In general, the purpose of a sitcom premise is to contrive a way that people who don't particularly like each other, or who generate conflict when in close proximity, can be forced to occupy the same space for the duration of a plot. Over time, TV sitcom has settled on two or three ways of doing this effectively: using a family unit (e.g. *The Simpsons*), using employment where people can't escape the same workplace (e.g. *Futurama*), or sometimes doing both at once (e.g. *Bob's Burgers*).

Similarly, horror plots require characters to be unable to leave their immediate situation. Characters might be physically stuck in a dangerous location; for example, the infested ships, collapsed colonies, or remote foundry-prisons of the *Alien* franchise – or they might be pinned in a situation under the sheer weight of etiquette; for example, the 'meet the family' set-up of *Get Out* (2017), or the 'please the boss' set-up of *Sorry to Bother You* (2018).

So how does sci-fi tie in? If both comedy and horror benefit from characters being trapped like spiders in a bathtub, the tropes of sci-fi offer loads of really interesting ways in which to do that trapping. They can be marooned in spaceships (e.g. *Red Dwarf*), snared in extra-terrestrial job postings (e.g. *Moon*), or flung into time periods that aren't their own (e.g. parts of *The Hitchhikers' Guide to the Galaxy*). All of which are not only difficult situations to escape, but also the kind of load-bearing settings which support interesting worldbuilding and plot.

Suggestion Two: In both horror and comedy, the characters' attempts to fix their situation make everything worse

Mechanically, both horror and comedy plots tend to hinge on protagonists actively struggling against adversity... and making things far worse in the process. In *Alien* (spoiler alert, but you've had since 1979 to watch it...) Ripley is faced by something fast and hungry, and quite keen to eat the remaining crew of the *USCSS Nostromo*. Her solution? Retreat to the shuttle, and blow up the *Nostromo* with the alien on it. Ripley retreats, and the *Nostromo* self-destructs. The result? Ripley realises that the alien followed her to the shuttle, and she still has the problem, but now has no ship, and no surviving colleagues. It's beat-for-beat the plot logic that appears in shows like *The Simpsons* week after week – a character ends up in hot water, attempts to fix it with lies, improv, a change of vocation, or a musical number, and ends up in even hotter water as a result.

So how does sci-fi tie in? It offers a palette of tools and technologies to make characters' plights significantly worse at scale. Think you've made things better? Your mistakes can ripple disastrously across multiverses (as in many episodes of *Rick and Morty*). Think you've averted a crisis? Your actions can sprawl across time (as in Ray Bradbury's *A Sound of Thunder*). Think you've fixed a relationship? You haven't – and it's affecting *Everything, Everywhere, All at Once*. The kind of failure-cascades that sci-fi supports work brilliantly for both comedy and horror plots, and for elevating stakes from personal to existential.

Suggestion Three: Both horror and comedy benefit from unhelpful, intransigent weirdos

Structurally, a lot of comedy works by having a 'straight' protagonist surrounded by, and slightly disconnected from, a world of colourful, heightened, eccentric characters. The protagonist succeeds in their goals despite, not because of, the actions of those around them. In *The Simpsons*, Lisa often attempts to work around her brother's mischief, her father's sloth/ignorance/anger/gluttony, and her mother's ineffective support.

In horror, you tend to get a very similar set-up; a 'normal' protagonist is alert to, and aware of, the dangers of the central threat, but surrounded by, and disarticulated from, a cast of heightened characters who are either indifferent or complicit. In Alien, Ripley has to work around Mother, Bishop, Weyland Yutani, and her increasingly panicked, edible colleagues.

So how does sci-fi tie in? On the one hand, the tropes of sci-fi offer a whole host of unhelpful, heightened character-types with which to populate a piece. You can have robots/androids/AIs/replicants who operate on intransigent, inscrutable, or actively harmful logics; it's possible to compare Arthur C Clarke's HAL 9000, Grant and Naylor's Holly and Kryten, Douglas Adams' Marvin, and Harlan Ellison's AM – that automated incompetence or obstinacy can be played either for comedy or for horror. You can also have alien characters who are incomprehensible or positioned vertically on the food chain; Xenomorphs and Vogons are found respectively in horror and in comedy, but mechanically they're fulfilling the same function. On the other hand, sci-fi premises also offer a variety of effective ways in which to jolt the narrator-protagonist away from their surrounding cast; in *The Day of the Triffids* (1951) John Wyndam's protagonist becomes separated from the majority of the world by his personal history of Triffid-husbandry, and a well-timed hospital visit in the face of a 'meteor shower'. In JG Ballard's The Secret History of World War 3 (1988, a bit of stunning, and worryingly prescient, satire), the jolt for

the narrator is equally unsettling, but played in the opposite direction, for laughs. So sci-fi offers not just a variety of eccentric and unusual character-types, but also a great toolkit of ways to isolate the central character from those that surround them.

In addition, both comedy and horror paradoxically thrive simultaneously on a sense of shock/surprise and a common (between author/director and reader/viewer) understanding of formula. Both seek immediate, visceral reactions. Both require static characters who can't and don't learn, remaining as misfortune 'sponges', mopping up everything that's thrown at them. Both involve consciously deciding what to reveal and what to conceal from the audience, and deciding what to let the reader/viewer/listener conclude on their own, filling in the gaps.

Why does it matter if comedy and horror are made from the same ingredients? The similarities enable writers to do some very fun things because if the boundary between comedy and horror is porous, writers can choose to switch between the two genres, or to do both simultaneously.

Possibility One: Genre-switching for effect

The ability to subtly push something from being comedy to being horror (and vice versa) means that writers can choose to playfully hop across the boundary, for deliberate effect. For example; *Inside No. 9 writers* Reece Shearsmith and Steve Pemberton seem to enjoy swerving from one tone to the other, or sometimes purposely leaving the genre of the piece unresolved at the start – so the viewer is disorientated, trying to work out whether they should be laughing or just feeling tense at the misfortune unfolding onscreen. Similarly, Chuck Palahniuk plays a brilliant trick in a lot of his shorter fiction, where a piece will start comic, and gradually twist itself into something darker – meaning that (a) the reader is lulled into a sense of security so the grotesqueness hits all the harder, and (b) the reader feels complicit with the disturbing things that the narrator goes on to do and/or experience, having laughed along at the start (with his 2004 short story 'Guts' perhaps offering the archetype of the structural trick...).

Possibility Two: Buy-One-Get-One-Free

Secondly, I think the mechanical similarities between comedy and horror mean that if a writer wants to flavour their sci-fi with both comedy and horror, it's almost a 'buy-one-get-one-free' situation – that the same set-up facilitates both payoffs, with no extra word-count. Personally, the comedic sci-fi that I enjoy most also tends to lean into the horrific elements of their set-ups. So *Red Dwarf* is both an excellent workplace comedy (Rimmer and Lister are bickering colleagues who can't stand each other but also can't escape each other), and an excellent deep-space horror (Lister is the last human alive, effectively stranded a very long time and space away from anyone who once knew him, and his only company is a hologram of his dead bunkmate who was killed in a grisly industrial accident, a slightly broken mechanoid, an unhelpful ship's computer, and the thing which evolved from the things which evolved from his cat).

Equally, Terry Gilliam's *Brazil* (1985) is quite a disarming blend of different types of comedy and different types of horror – all of which emerge from the same set-ups. The world of Brazil is one in which a large, inefficient, and vindictive bureaucracy is large, inefficient, and vindictive. This supports all sorts of different registers of comedy - from cerebral satire, Tom Stoppard-y wordplay, and silly physical slapstick (petty bureaucrats play tug-of-war with desks installed down the middle of partition walls), while on the other hand, the set-up also supports visceral horror elements (with the bureaucracy violently abducting citizens, subjecting them to various itemised interrogation procedures, and keeping meticulous records of everything said, screamed, and whimpered) at the same time as slow, claustrophobic horror (with a creeping sense of unease, as the net of the inflexible system slowly closes around the protagonist, like a feeding Venus Fly Trap). Personally, I think that the genius of Brazil is in layering all of those elements together; swerving from slapstick to body horror, from cerebral wordy jokes into implied violence – heightening both the humour and the horror of the scenes (and really making the most, both comedically and horrifically, from every worldbuilding detail introduced).

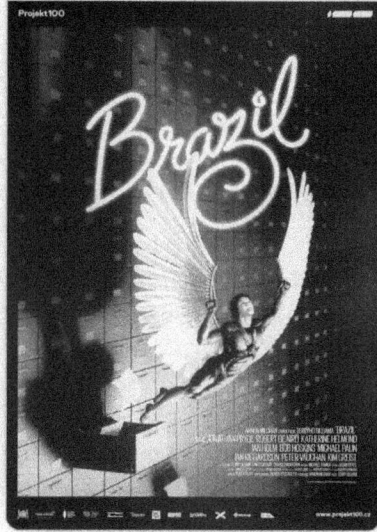

So, in conclusion, I think that comedy and horror are broadly made from the same ingredients, since both require characters that are (a) trapped, (b) trying desperately to escape their problems, and making them worse in the process, and (c) surrounded by, but somehow separated from, other characters who obstruct them. I also think that the palette of sci-fi tropes very naturally lend themselves to supporting these facets, and that it's time to rewatch Brazil, time to sew the frog back up, disinfect the scalpel, and dismantle the metaphor.

Emma Levin is a writer of comedy, sci-fi, and comedy sci-fi. Her short stories have appeared in anthologies (e.g. The Best of British Science Fiction 2019 & 2021), in magazines (e.g. *Shoreline of Infinity*), and online (e.g. *Daily Science Fiction*). She received training in writing for broadcast through the BBC's 'Comedy Room' Writers' Scheme, and some of her jokes have turned up on the radio and in video games.

SHORELINE OF INFINITY

Shoreline of Infinity's Event Horizon: live, online and on Youtube.

www.youtube.com/@shorelineofinfinity

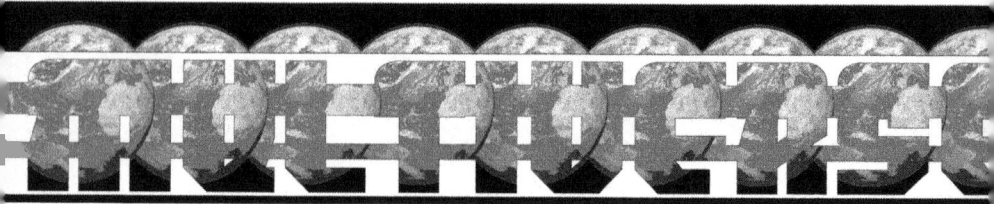

Evidence to the Committee (Closed Session)

Judith Taylor

It was lovely work. A horse is sleek
but picture the sleekest horse you can imagine
and make it more so. The hide like eelskin
faintly slimed, and glimmering under moonlight;
the musculature both stripped down
(to reduce the drag in water), and enhanced for strength.

It was sinuous. The long head
little changed; the intelligent, dark-adapted eye;
the shark teeth. No, I don't recall the rationale
behind that choice in particular, but we knew
it wouldn't be capable of what we had in mind for it
on a plant-based diet. We built a predator
for bursts of strength and speed.
The beauty was incidental.

Less so when a few got out of course.
It's intelligent, as I noted, and it knows humans
(yes, the lab team first) have a sentimental streak
for what some poet called *that long-
lost archaic companionship.*
It plays on that. Imagine

the most beautiful horse you ever saw
apparently grazing - strayed, perhaps -
by a river-side, at twilight.
Of course you approach it, talking softly, steadily

so it won't spook: when you're close enough,
reach out a hand to stroke its powerful neck.
The head comes up, and

that's you gone.
It sucks the blood at the point of killing
so there's little trace. And it's realised
the pool below a waterfall
is the perfect place for a larder of the parts
it will eat at leisure, later

- with the additional advantage
of the accidental drownings. No,
I'm not trying to minimise the death toll,
but some of the lost were lost
to misadventure. To skinny-dipping
drunkenly, on a bright night.
It doesn't balk at carrion.

I understand the necessity of course
for it to be hunted to extinction now. We can't risk
the establishment of a breeding population
or any spread to the Lowlands, and the towns.
I think there are lessons here for all of us.
I hope, however, the record will reflect

the full extent of the team's
scientific achievement: the groundwork
they have laid down
for the next tranche of experiments
to address this brief. Let the minutes show
what lovely work it was.

WRT Surface Habitation & Operations

Judith Taylor

It's the old story. Young and inexperienced agents mostly,
who think they're in love.
Remember that awful tale that came out of Hjaltland
- the one who fathered a child, and tried to take it home,
and the husband shot them both?

More often, though, it's women:
beguiled at first, then trapped. Coerced.
As if holding someone against her will
and beating her if she looks for the way to leave again
is a marriage. I don't care how you try to explain it.
    They're barbarians.

It's lost in the data somewhere,
the process by which the teams diverged.
Something to do with catastrophic events upside
no doubt. There are plenty of candidates:
pandemics, earthquakes; all the major eruptions
to have darkened the sun. It's sad

and a little frightening
how easily S.H.O. reverted to ignorance
and superstition. I'm sorry, but really
what else can you call it? Centuries of technical evolution, all forgotten.
They frame our applications now as magic,
we who use them as uncanny

even dangerous. In their archaeology
we appear as the Sea Peoples: inexplicable, hostile, and destructive.
But more often we're mythology
adorned sometimes with spurious gills or fish-tails
or conflated with some marine mammal.

The symbiosuit persists in a few of their stories
as a skin that can be doffed and donned

for switching between the elements. It's that core of truth
that makes the legend dangerous.
They remember enough to know that if they hide the skin, or destroy it,
the owner's trapped on-shore until they find it again.
Or else forever.

This case right now in the Hebrides.
We are monitoring closely, within security constraints of course.
We know, and now the agent knows
for sure, poor soul, that we cannot risk
the descendants of the people who were our colleagues long ago
learning the truth any more.

Our way of life, our cities, would be endangered.
But let me assure you
Subsea Exploration and Living-space Command
will not abandon its personnel
to neo-primitive patriarchy and exploitation.

Teams are watching his every move
trying to help her find the suit
(there's this to say for ignorant fear - they very rarely burn it)
and bring her home.
We are up there, signalling to her, nightly

- that's low-risk for discovery. They only hear
in a narrow range of wavelengths
and they find it weirdly enchanting.
Some of them come right down to the water's edge
and play their fiddles back again
as if they could understand us.
As if our grief was singing.

Judith Taylor lives and works in Aberdeen, where she is one of the organisers of the monthly Poetry at Books and Beans events. Her first full-length collection, *Not in Nightingale Country*, is published by Red Squirrel Press, and she is one of the Editors of Poetry Scotland magazine.
http://sometimesjudy.co.uk/

Lessons in Seismology

Morgan L. Ventura

Earth shook Mexico City September 19, 1985
twisting city innards, devastating water supplies.
Popocatépetl loomed against neon sky,
spitting smoke on the horizon.

It happened again exactly 32 years later,
a sort of lesson in seismology
or, perhaps, cosmology.

As cement rained down and screams sliced air,
the roaming abyss of the earth's belly
made itself known. A traffic light leapt into the park,

melting into ravished earth,
while historians reminded everyone:
'we built a city on a swamp
on the edge of a tectonic plate.'

Which is to say that Tenochtitlán
was a terrible idea
even if it was ordained.

Amidst the tyranny of raging stone,
I caught the earth's ruby eye peering up at me
from its conflagrated nest nestled
between crumbling crust, jagged edges.

Eye inside jaws inside belly inside beast.
Its trembling could be laughter,
I thought, so I bent down on my knees
to ask our shaking hearth,

'What kind of god are you?'
and the earth shot back,
'What kind of god are you!'

Human ingenuity is dreaming the outrageous
or forbidden, hands and minds stubborn eternal.
Which is to say, Mexico City sinks
twenty inches every year.

Bag Tag No. 048

Morgan L. Ventura

Field Museum of Natural History
PROYECTO LA FORTALEZA DE MITLA

Material: *Bone / Hueso*

Site Name / Nombre del sitio: *La Fortaleza de Mitla*

Provenience: *Platform 4, Unit 12C*

Date / Fecha : *04-21-2010*

Name / Nombre : *GMF*

Notes / Notas:

I take the bone to my tongue,
lick its parched skin
to discern whether it's bone or pottery.
That's how you do archaeology, you see?
You must know when to use every part
of your body. My hands plummet into soil,
my fingers trace old wounds, scarified bones.
Violent hands of another ossified, immortalized.
This is how we become haunted.
Inside the burial, a fieldworker faints.
Overhead the sun screeches, and I unhinge
her gentle jaws. Coral tongue shrivels,
floating, lizard-like. Did you know
the tongue contains no bones?

Morgan L. Ventura is a poet, writer, and curator based between Belfast and Oaxaca. A former archaeologist, their poetry and short fiction have appeared or are forthcoming in T*he Magazine of Fantasy and Science Fiction*, *Strange Horizons*, *Augur*, and *Lackington's*. You can find Morgan on Twitter: @hmorganvl

Cyborgs

Anna Idelevich

Yes? Then I want to be a cyborg. Sensors, light sparkles - for the fuck. When trying to resist, she takes out a mythical weapon, sprinkles with glass fragments, they go out. The design of the filming hall changes, darkness, then light, then twilight. Space music sounds conciliatory. The actor spat. Rain poured down in silver glittering threads. Half the distance covered, but he hasn't touched it yet. He is big and she is small. Corrosion of alloys goes from the neck to the hemispheres of the chest. The nipples are small, just in the slot of his fingers. Numerous face of large width under the fly. Its structure exceeds its structure - it is advisable to give time. Or forget the time? A catastrophe is inevitable for the personal museum of the heart... Then suddenly she falls down and falls into the arms of another cyborg. No liquid, no gas, nothing around, just a warm, warm big hand. It is impossible to look more carefully, it acts quickly. Wet between the legs. Everything is felt. Then meat, tongue, saliva.

Aaaa ... cattle ...

Anna Idelevich is a scientist by profession, Ph.D., MBA, trained in the neuroscience field at Harvard University. She writes poetry for pleasure. Her books and poetry collections include "DNA of the Reversed River" and "Cryptopathos" published by the Liberty Publishing House, NY.

Anna's poems were featured in *Louisville Review, BlazeVOX, The Racket, New Contrast, Zoetic press, Hawaii Pacific Review, Cholla Needles* of among others. We hope you will enjoy their melody, new linguistic tone, and a slight tint of an accent.

Once Upon a Biofuture: Tales for a New Millennium is an anthology of stories, from fiction to memoir, by a multidisciplinary team of scientists in the UK Centre for Mammalian Biology at The University of Edinburgh

A mix of biology, philosophy and mythology, they explore a powerful new technology that is re-engineering our world: synthetic biology. Many of the stories are biographical, offering insight into how the scientists become scientists and the lessons learned through science exploration, or taking us to new imaginative worlds

The stories were recorded and transcribed, or workshopped and edited by Jessica Fox, former storyteller for NASA, and artist-in-residence at the Centre. This unique role enabled the scientists to lead the storytelling and retain creative control while being guided by an experienced writer.

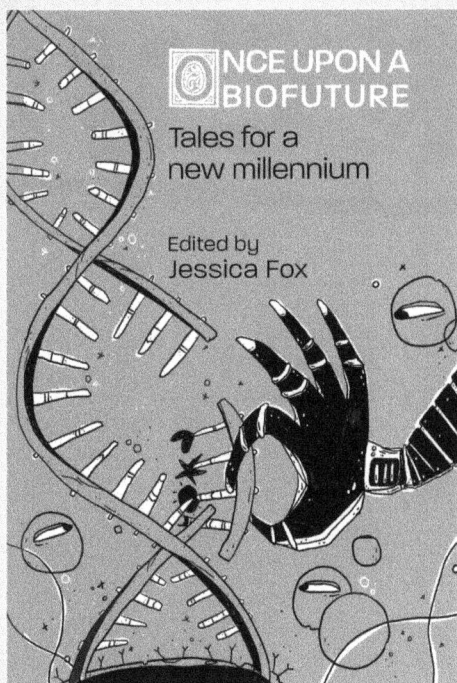

ONCE UPON A BIOFUTURE
Tales for a new millennium

Edited by Jessica Fox

Once Upon a Biofuture: Tales for a new millennium
Edited by Jessica Fox
Published by The New Curiosity Shop/ Shoreline of Infinity Publications
ISBN: 978-1-7396736-6-6
RRP: £12.00

Stories from Science...

...is what happens when you gather scientists and writers together.

To find out more and discuss your ideas visit:

www.shorelineofinfinity.com/storiesfromscience

Sistersong

Lucy Holland

Published by Pan Macmillan in April 2021

Review by Veronika Groke

Three sisters, different in character and ambition.

One kingdom, threatened by a powerful enemy from without, and the spread of a new religion displacing the old beliefs from within.

Lucy Holland's historical fantasy novel *Sistersong* added a British angle to a lineup of many excellent retellings of classic myths with female central characters published in recent years (such as Madeline Miller's *Circe*, Natalie Haynes's *A Thousand Ships*, and Jennifer Saint's *Ariadne*). In it, Holland takes on the not insubstantial task of telling a story of epic proportions in no fewer than three different narrative voices. Disfigured by a childhood accident, embittered Riva grapples with ever stronger feelings of her own inadequacy as she sees her one talent, a gift for healing through magic, repressed by the Christian priest who has gained a hold over her royal parents. Barely having outgrown childhood, playful Sinne dreams of romance and does her best to ignore the conflict building up around her. Sombre, boyish Keyne, meanwhile, longs to take her part in it – but not in the role that's been staked out for her by society.

Holland's development and structuring of the storyline is incredibly clever. While the plot is based on seventeenth-century murder ballad 'The Twa Sisters', Holland transplants it

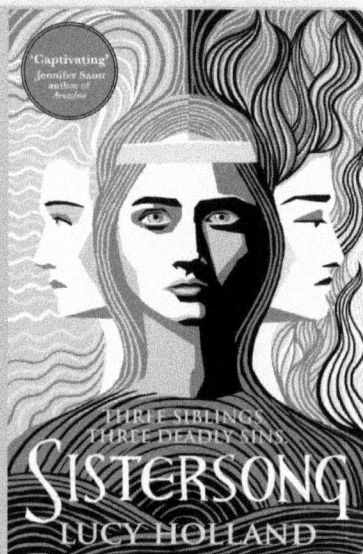

to sixth-century Dumnonia, a kingdom in southwestern Britain, and peoples it with a mixture of characters from British history and myth. Gildas, the zealous priest intent on converting the British infidels, and his adversary, the Dumnonian king Constantine, are both historical figures whose stories are closely bound up with Arthurian legend. Holland exploits the many vaguenesses surrounding this 'mythistory' to dramatic effect, filling in the gaps in the historical record with rich detail derived from other sources. The different parts of the book are structured around Celtic and Germanic pre-Christian festivals such as Imbolc, Lammas, and Yule, thereby providing a focus for the characters' day-to-day activities and containing the story in a narrative framework that echoes the protagonists' struggle against the new faith being imposed on them.

Stylistically, I had some difficulties to fully get into the story at first. While there is no reason an ancient tale shouldn't be told in a contemporary style (as, for example, in Pat Barker's celebrated *The Silence of the Girls*), the tone of *Sistersong's* narrative voices never quite settles between 'archaic' and 'modern', which initially had the effect of frequently jarring me out of the story. Likewise, the immediacy of the present tense (though well-suited to the dramatic nature of the plot) at times works to undermine the narrators' credibility by bestowing a little too much self-awareness on them. I personally also found the depiction of magic in the novel too cinematic. Silver threads sprout from Keyne's fingers, and the scenes conjured by wizard Myrdhin's storytelling appear in the royal hall as if on a screen. Towards the end, one of the characters undergoes a transformation whose detailed description, though true to the source material (i.e., the various versions of the 'Twa Sisters' murder ballad), felt rather implausible.

In the end, however, the pattern Holland weaves out of her various story yarns adds up to a tapestry so vivid it can withstand the odd flash of silver. The voices of the three sisters, each quite distinctive and with its own point of view, alternate perfectly to drive the narrative along at a consistently fast pace. The characters themselves are compellingly three-dimensional; rather than straight-out 'goodies' or 'baddies', what we get are complex individuals capable of making mistakes and changing their minds. Holland had me hooked with the appearance of the enigmatic Tristan, a character as inscrutable as he is handsome: is he the promised husband of Sinne's dreams? – Riva's unexpected soulmate? – or the harbinger of death and destruction Keyne suspects him to be? Or are things, perhaps, not quite as simple as any of these?

The character who ultimately completely won me over, however, was Keyne. In the interest of avoiding spoilers for anyone who hasn't read it yet, let me just say that, while all the sisters' stories are gripping, watching sullen Keyne finally come into their own actually sent shivers down my spine. To make a long story short, Holland is one hell of a storyteller, and I am very excited to be reading her new novel *Song of the Huntress* next, which is out this month.

Dragonfall

L.R. Lam

Part 1 of the Dragon Scales Trilogy
Published May 2023 by
Hodderscape (Hodder & Stoughton)
Reviewed by Samantha Dolan

It has been a long time since I've read anything fantasy, so it took me a few chapters for my mind to accept the general vibe of the story.

As a high-level summary, this is a story of two main characters. Everen is the last male dragon, living beyond the Veil with his mother and sister under the weight of a 'society saving' prophecy. When an impatient Everen grows tired of the accusing stares of the other dragons, he takes matters into his own hands and pierces the veil between their land and the human world. When he arrives, he is met in the storm by a human called Arcady who is in the process of stealing a magical seal from a tomb. It transpires that the connection between the two is the key to Everen fulfilling his prophecy. In order to get enough magic to let the dragons back into the world, stolen from them by the humans long ago, Everen needs to make sure Arcady trusts him.

I had a bit of a tricky time with the narrative position. Everen is telling the story to Arcady, but at the same time Arcady is telling the story in the third person - and it can be a little jarring when Everen starts to refer to 'you' but Arcady doesn't use the first person. I kept wondering why Everen was talking to Arcady, particularly when they are sharing the same space and time. There's something awkward in the second person narrative position that isn't resolved when Arcady takes over the narration.

Lam spends a lot of time emphasising the gender neutrality of the human word. There are signs for the pronouns and we're told it's impolite to assume a gender before being told. Through Everen, the reader starts to understand that expectation. But we're introduced to this earlier with a capitalised 'They' which made it

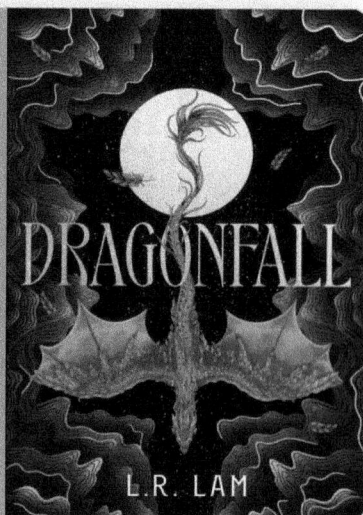

clear that pronouns were a large consideration in this society. I personally felt the exposition disenfranchised the reader but I can also accept that Lam is writing for a wide audience and pronoun concepts are still taking root in wider society.

I think the biggest strength of *Dragonfall* is the writing. I've read several of Lam's other novels and this one certainly feels like an evolution. Lam's prose is beautiful and the amount of dedication to world building really pays off. Lovers of this genre will have plenty to sink their teeth into and luxuriate as this first of the trilogy is takes time and care in worldbuilding and character development.

I suspect it's intentional, considering the importance of their connection, that the two protagonists sound so similar, but as a result I did find the romantic portions harder to get into. I would have found it more interesting for them to build bonds of siblinghood and see how that played out instead.

In part, *Dragonfall* reads more like Young Adult fiction, which would be historically on brand for Lam, but there is still maturity in the narrative. For me, the exposition about the way the society works and all the calls back beyond the Vale removed some of the tension. It read smoothly but without huge emotional investment. It hasn't sold me on the Romantasy genre but I'm definitely intrigued by the scope of the world Lam is building, and I'm looking forward to the next instalment.

Equinox

Ruth Aylett and Greg Michaelson

Published by Stairwell Books in May 2023

Pages 230

Reviewed by Moira McPartlin

Helen (Hulkie) McIver's survey vessel drags a body from the waters around the Outer Hebrides. As ship's engineer and medic, she gets more than she bargains for when she pockets a compelling green stone she finds on the corpse.

In a dual narrative, Helen's cousin Malcolm, a ranger with Rural Resources, finds a similar stone after an encounter with a strange woman carrying a broken arrowhead talisman. Nearby on Rannoch Moor, a high-tech company, Fundamental Forces (F^2), is researching a new form of green energy.

The body's enquiry takes Helen to Lewis, where she is confronted by an F^2 operative and at the Callanish Stones encounters a mystical old woman who wears an arrowhead talisman and utters a strange prophecy.

"I couldn't shake off the feeling he'd somehow been following me. Something to do with the pebble? I fished it out yet again and stared at it. It didn't look engineered, just sea-smoothed."

The F^2 connection leads Helen to Rannoch Moor and her cousin. When they begin to compare notes, the list of coincidences mount.

As the plot flips back and forward between the alternating

stories of Helen and Malcolm, a connection emerges involving The Wicca, a pagan cult of witches who are identified by their arrowhead talisman. The talisman, worn by many local women known to Malcolm, is made from calc-silicate hornfel and sourced at Creag Na Cailliach Quarry in Killin, a meeting place of these women at the Equinox.

"Glenys popped the arrowhead into the hat and muttered a few words. Then she reached into the hat and drew out a very small grey rabbit."

The cousins suspect something sinister is happening at the F^2 plant. Who are the two Americans who visited Malcolm just before his cottage is ransacked? The same Americans Helen overhears talking about the Rannoch Moor plant, transilience gates and quantum wave packets.

On the surface, the novel is a straightforward thriller to work through and uncover clues. But it is more than that. Scottish myth blends with science fiction.

One of the enjoyable aspects of the book is the locations used to create an authentic backdrop to the action; the Outer Hebrides, Rannoch Moor, Crianlarich, Loch Lomond, Loch Fyne and Kilmartin. There are many more entertaining characteristics to *Equinox,* not least that it is great fun to read - and there is a reason for that.

The co-authors wrote *Equinox* during the second lockdown in 2020. Although they live only a few streets apart, the pandemic kept them distant. They met on WhatsApp, developing initial storylines, settings, and plot elements. They then, independently, worked out their own protagonist and backstory, but collaborated on family connections. Working to a timetable, they wrote alternate chapters in the first person and shared summaries to keep each other informed. For the few joint chapters where Helen and Malcolm work together, authors Aylett and Michaelson set up WhatsApp video calls and wrote in real time.

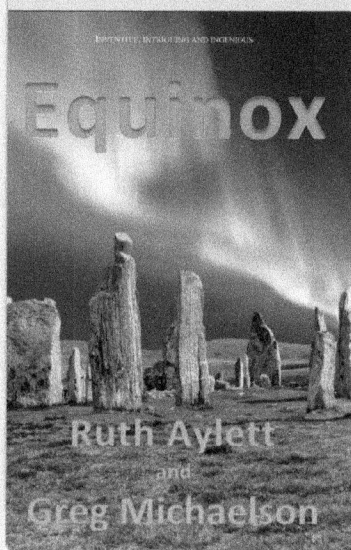

Both authors have collaborated in projects in the past. They are both Professors of Computer Science at Heriot Watt University, so there is no doubt that the science in the book is accurate. What comes across strongly in the reading of *Equinox* is just how much fun they had during the writing process.

Unlike other Sci-Fi novels, *Equinox* exudes joy. The characters are flawed and believable; Helen, big bossy who finds lying comes easy to her, and Malcom, the reluctant hero who wants to be left alone in his ranger world.

There are many character tropes that appear deliberate; the hapless local bobby and his seductive wife Glenys, the two American professors with their *Man in Black* style goons, the enthusiastic activist and his sensible wife, witches' cats.

Other devices at play too: The use of the colour green; stones, cats' eyes, green energy. The use of word play; Rural Resources, Fundamental Forces, Creag Na Caillich Quarry where Cailleach is a variant of the Gaelic for old hag. The authors threw them all in, and it works.

This novel is Wickerman meets His Dark Materials with the humour of Discworld. It is quirky, clever and layered with hidden meaning. Give yourself a treat with a little slice of joy.

Writing the Future
Edited by Dan Coxton and Richard V. Hirst
Published by Dead Ink Books in September 2023
Reviewed by Lisa Timpf

I haven't come across many books that made me feel as though my brain had been stretched, but that's the sensation I had after reading *Writing the Future: Essays on Crafting Science Fiction*. Edited by Dan Coxon and Richard V. Hirst. *Writing the Future* offers 13 chapters organized into three sections: "Imagined Futures," "The Worst is Yet to Come," and "Building Rockets and Landing on Planets." Though linked by the over-arching theme of writing about the future, the chapters were sufficiently varied in content to keep things interesting.

As someone who has written a few short stories that might be termed climate fiction, I found " 'It's about to get crazy, it's about to get loud': Weird Ecopoetics at the End of the World" by Marian Womack very relevant. Womack discusses the difficulties in getting people to buy into the realities of climate change, and at the same time, offers strategies for getting the point across. Womack argues that some of the most powerful eco-fiction is written with surreal or uncanny elements.

I'm a fan of Una McCormack's fiction – in *Star Trek: Picard – The Last Best Hope*, McCormack portrayed Jean-Luc Picard exactly as I had always pictured him – so I was quite interested in her piece titled " 'Right now the building is ours': Affinities of Science Fiction and Historical Fiction." McCormack notes that "the stretch between past and future – between writing historical fiction and writing science fiction – is not, I think, too far," and discusses how writing tie-in novels shares similarities with historical fiction.

"A Crash Course in Black Holes" by Aliya Whiteley depicts the challenges of finding the right balance between learning enough background information to write about a topic, and falling down a rabbit-hole of research. It's a theme I'm all too familiar with, having misspent many happy hours in the library in my graduate student days following breadcrumb trails to satisfy my curiosity when I should have been more focussed. Entertainingly written, this chapter also includes some important insights.

Three of the chapters, one per section, focus on one particular author's writings. Anne Charnock writes about Margaret Atwood, mainly discussing *The Handmaid's Tale* while referencing some of Atwood's other works as well. Adam Roberts explores H. G. Wells' writing, delving into the way Wells' worldview and themes changed at different periods in his life. Nina Allan discusses the impact J. G. Ballard's writings had on her. In each of these cases, the articles' authors showed an in-depth knowledge of the author's work.

In "The Novel of the Future," Oliver K. Langmead discusses writers who are "doing some extraordinary things" with the novel form, providing examples like Mark Z. Danielewski's *House of Leaves* and Rian Hughes' *XX*. Elsewhere in *Writing the Future*, readers are treated to a background look at the British comic *2000 AD* and Judge Dredd, musings about

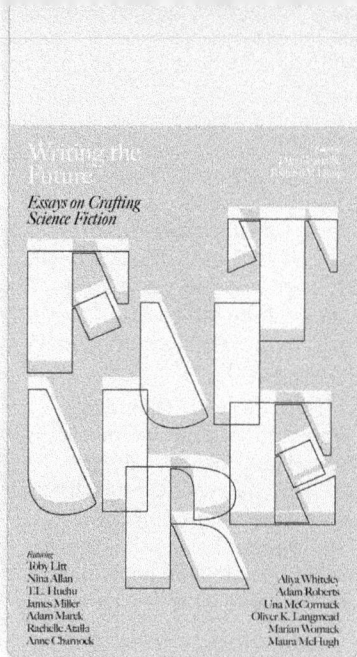

what the future really is, and the difficulties of writing about truly "alien" aliens, as well as other topics. *Writing the Future* contains just shy of 170 footnotes. At the end of the book, a list of 100 recommended speculative novels and 50 speculative short stories is provided as fodder for the reading list.

Writing the Future's introduction suggests that one of the roles of speculative fiction is to "create a map of the future by which we might better navigate the present." Exploring a broad range of topics, including the nature of the future, the future of the novel, and novel ways of writing dystopias, *Writing the Future* provides an appetizing buffet of interesting, insightful, and thought-provoking pieces for readers and writers of speculative fiction.

Reviews are also published online at
www.shorelineofInfinity.com

SF CALEDONIA

Wanted:

SF stories by Scottish Writers

What can I submit?

We're looking for stories that have already been published somewhere in the world. Not self-published, or on your own website.

We would love to see contributions in any of the Scottish languages and dialects.

Accepted authors will also be asked to provide a short biography, public contact details (web, social media) and links to where readers can buy their books. This will be posted alongside the story, and be searchable through the website.

Who is a Scottish Writer?

You were born, lived or live in Scotland. The exact criteria are on the website.

Is there a payment?

There will be a small reprint fee. If we can attract funding, that will be increased.

Are you looking for help?

SF Caledonia is purely volunteer driven. If you are interested in helping in any capacity, contact the Editor through the website.

Ideas and Suggestions

SF Caledonia is a new model, and we are looking for ideas and suggestions on how to develop it. Do get in touch with your thoughts (especially if you are in a position to help develop your suggestions).

Online showcase for Scottish science fiction & fantasy

www.sfcaledonia.scot

CYMERA

SCOTLAND'S FESTIVAL OF SCIENCE FICTION, FANTASY & HORROR WRITING

SAVE THE DATE
FOR #CYMERA2024
31 MAY - 2 JUNE 2024

IN EDINBURGH AND ONLINE
WWW.CYMERAFESTIVAL.CO.UK

SHORELINE OF INFINITY

Awar
Winn
Scier
Fictic

Shoreline of Infinity is based in Edinburgh, Scotland, and began life in 2015.

Shoreline of Infinity Science Fiction Magazine is a print and digital magazine published quarterly in PDF, ePub and Kindle formats. It features new short stories, poetry, art, reviews and articles.

But there's more – we run regular live science fiction events called Event Horizon, with a whole mix of science fiction related entertainments such as story and poetry readings, author talks, music, drama, short films – we've even had sword fighting.

We also publish a range of science fiction related books; take a look at our collection at the Shoreline Shop. You can also pick up back copies of all of our issues.Details on our website...

www.shorelineofinfinity.com

Milton Keynes UK
Ingram Content Group UK Ltd.
UKHW021609210524
442961UK00009B/99